MINNI[...] E
AT[...]

Cyril Kersh

A CRESCENT BOOK
Published by the Hardback Division of
W. H. ALLEN & Co. PLC

First published by
W. H. Allen & Co. Ltd, 1979

Crescent edition published in 1987

Set by Galleon Photosetting, Ipswich
Printed and bound in Great Britain by
Biddles Ltd, Guildford, Surrey
for the publishers, W. H. Allen & Co. Plc
44 Hill Street, London W1X 8LB

ISBN 0 427 00059 9

For Suzanne

ONE

With much groaning and wheezing protest, my mother lowered herself to the edge of my father's grave, gave me an accusing look and said: 'I hope this isn't damp. On top of arthritis, that's all I'm short of: rheumatism.' She sighed, looked down and plucked at the grass that grew from between the granite chippings. Absently: 'Not that it can be so nice for you, either, may you rest in peace.' Then, as the tears came, she looked up at me and jerked her head in a gesture of dismissal. 'Go away, busybody. Hop it. Go mind your own business. I want a private conversation. Go aggravate someone else.'

I shrugged and moved to a grave in the next plot, the wording on its headstone assuring me that Abraham Tulip (1860–1926) would be remembered and mourned to all eternity by his sorrowing wife, children, grandchildren, nephews, cousins, in-laws and friends. This sentiment was readable only when I'd scraped away weeds, ivy, bird droppings and dirt – whereupon the headstone fell face forward and with a thunderous crash shattered upon the moss-carpeted tomb beneath.

The fright of the sudden noise brought a shrill scream from my mother, followed in Yiddish by: 'God save us all! Messiah has come! The dead are rising from their graves!' Then a long silence until, very slowly, her face peered from the side of my father's headstone. When she realized what had happened she shrieked and hurled handfuls of granite chippings at me. 'Madman! Cossack! Murderer! Assassin! Even the dead you can't leave in peace! Filth! . . .' When she was exhausted she managed a final 'Stinkpot!' and moved out of sight again . . .

'So you can see what I've got to put up with. A madman in the family (although God alone knows who he takes after). A son who desiccated graves. So is it right? Is it fair? Isn't it enough being a widow and now, with a war started, having to give up my home and move? . . . Mind you, I could have stayed in Kilburn. Oh yes.' (I could visualize her vehement head-nodding.) 'I could have stayed all right. But with Mother and Mendel and all the rest in the East End, it seemed safer if we were all together. You follow me? . . . It was hard to know what to do for the best, mind you. Which way to turn. It wasn't as though you were here to advise (may you rest happy in

Paradise). But Mendel said that to move stood to reason. Was logic.

'Mind you, you do *feel* safer now we're all together, if you follow me. When you know what's happening you don't worry about what might have happened. And to tell you the truth, I owed so much to the landlord and the fishmonger and the lousy butcher (may his boils also have boils) I wasn't sorry to do a flit.

'So anyway, I've come like I always do before the Day of Atonement. I know I usually come a bit nearer the time, but this year, with a war on, and everyone likely to be bombed to smithereens in their beds, there's going to be a lot of visiting and repenting to catch up with, so I thought I'd come early and miss the rush. Not that *I've* got anything to repent mind you. You can set your mind at rest on that score . . . Oh no, I've done nothing to be ashamed of. Faults maybe I've got – that I admit. But how come sins? And I know my faults, which is more than can be said for certain others whose names I won't mention . . . At least not here.'

A long sigh. 'F'rinstance, I know I'm too soft-hearted, too good. But is that a sin? Have I done anything you might actually call bad? Eh, have I? So all right – the butcher. But wouldn't I have paid every penny I owe, and to spare, if I'd had the money? You know.

You can speak up for me . . . Well, maybe not here, but up there. In the Golden Book. So to feed the children is a sin all of a sudden?

'People have got to eat. I've got it on good authority.' Another sigh. 'If they didn't, we'd all be Rothschilds.

'So God wants I should starve them to death? . . . Mind you, why not? With all the other punishments he's wished on me, what's so extra about starvation? . . .'

I wandered off to mooch around the cemetery, past others in earnest monologue at the grave of a wife or husband; past a funeral and a stone-setting ceremony; then sat on a bench in the gritty sunshine – until my mother's shrill: 'So it's all right for you to enjoy yourself! Come and do what you came to do, you rotten toerag!'

I returned to my father's grave and recited the memorial prayer for the dead.

Even if one could have measured the sum of the chaos and heartache that the outbreak of war brought to the rest of the population, it would still have been of trifling account compared to the misery it brought to Minnie Ashe.

She shared the communal anguish at the thought of air raids and the recruitment of loved ones for their possible deaths; was apprehensive about the long-term effects of

genus. What else is he but genus?' She again addressed herself to the kitchen ceiling, more specifically that corner with the patch of damp where, as a small child, I'd supposed Heaven to be situated. 'Me, I've got no education. I was too busy working my fingers to the bone. So I still slave and sweat, and I'm also a widow (as you know full well). So isn't it marvellous: a mother can support two children, but two children can't support one mother. But what *can* they do? So I'll tell you. Criticize. That's what they can do. That's what they are also genuses at. Pick me up because I don't talk like the Duchess from Westminster . . . *Oi veh!*'

'But why *don't* you ask Uncle Mendel?' I persisted.

'Because I know what he'll say. In fact you were there. So now go and drive someone else potty, clever Dick.'

With my sister, Ruth, I had indeed been present at Zanzibar Terrace when my mother initially raised the matter. Uncle Mendel's advice had been: 'Relax, Minnie. Don't worry. The war's going to be over by Christmas. May God strike me dead and then paralyse me for life if I lie, but I saw this picture at the Troxy last week – the one with Lorry Oliver and Wassisname – and the weapons we got! You'd never believe. Tanks and guns and aeroplanes and whatsits. Them Germans – they'll never get nowhere. And don't forget them Frenchies have got their Magnetic Line.'

My mother frowned. 'Magnetic? Like with magnetism? So how does it work?'

Uncle Mendel was disconcerted for no more than ten seconds. He winked and tapped a finger against the side of his nose. 'It's what they call Top Secret – like in that newsreel that was also on at the Troxy. But it stands to reason: it's made of magnets, and with all the steel helmets and guns the *sheispot* Germans have got . . . You follow?'

'No,' said my mother flatly.

'Magnets, *shmagnets*,' said Granny Abrams. 'If you want my opinion, Minnie and the children should move in here. Like during the first war we was all together, and . . . well, like in the old days when the Cossacks came, we run away to hide among the trees, but before we run we was all together – and afterwards we was also all together. You understand me?'

'Sure I understand,' said my mother doubtfully.

On the bus back to Kilburn my mother made the inevitable remark about Aunt Zillah's cooking giving her heartburn, then sat in uncharacteristic silence until we were about to alight, when she muttered to herself rather than to anyone else: 'Mother says this. Mendel says the other. What's the answer?'

And that summed-up the underlying essence of my mother's misery: her inability to make a decision.

As she put it to her cronies as they sat variously peeling potatoes, shelling peas and darning socks under the elm tree in the centre of Daffodil Square: 'So I'm here. OK, there's mice and rats and men from the council and anti-semites (may they all suffer constipation for life), and I live in a basement flat that's so damp you don't need to go to the baths on Fridays – a soap and towel and you're spotless. So all right. But if the ceiling falls in on me, at least it's my own ceiling – or would be if it wasn't for the lousy landlord . . . So it isn't Paradise. It isn't the Palace from Buckingham, but it's my home. I've got mine independence. Of course I love my mother and brothers and people – it's only natural, no? Otherwise why would I be so worried? But to actually move in again with them after all these years . . .

'Yet again, my brother Mendel says it's going to be over by Christmas, please God. And he knows. He's the brains of the family. He meets people. Hears things. Goes regular to the pictures.'

'I haven't been to the pictures since I saw

Gordon Harker in "The Frog",' said Hettie Lewis. 'He also knew things.'

My mother sighed. 'The pictures . . . Al Jolson singing "Sonny Boy" . . . Aaah, them were the days.' She sniffed away near-tears. 'But suppose, just for the sake of argument, that Mendel was . . . well . . .' She looked about her as though fearful of Mendel's presence before she added, 'well . . . wrong.' She paled now, as though she'd uttered a dreadful blasphemy. 'Suppose the war isn't over? And there they are, while we're here. If only I knew what to do. I've prayed to God in Heaven, but it's like asking questions from a brick wall.'

Esther Cooperman: 'As my Leonard says, "Don't ask God too many questions or He might call for you to give you the answers personal." '

'God would do that, God forbid?' my mother cried, and spat three times to ward off the evil eye. Then, almost as an accusation: 'At least you've got a husband to give advice.'

Golda Kemensky, wearily: 'Can't you telephone?'

My mother stared at her. 'Telephone? What's with telephone? Since when have I got a telephone? . . . Telephone!' A short, contemptuous snort. 'I'm a millionaire, all of a sudden? So telephones are all right for the

King of England, for the Rothschilds. But for Minnie Ashe?'

'There's a box round the corner.'

'And suppose that gets bombed?'

Mrs Kemensky: 'There's another in Kilburn High Road.'

'And if that one also gets bombed? Or someone else is using it? What then? By the time I've finished running about in the middle of the night in my nightdress the war could be over, I'll have got double pneumonia and I still won't know from an answer.' She shrugged. 'Anyway, what's the use of wasting time talking about telephones?'

Hettie Lewis: 'Why should it be a waste of time? We're only trying to help.'

My mother snorted. 'It's a fat lot of help talking about telephones – Mendel hasn't got one.'

Pearl Weinberg clicked her teeth. 'No phone? Your brother Mendel? The big businessman?'

My mother shifted uncomfortably. Then, defiantly: 'He says he doesn't like the telephone for business. When he does a deal he likes to do it face to face. He says that when you're face to face, eye to eye, he can tell in a second if someone's a cheat or a liar. In a flash.' She snapped her fingers. 'Just like that.' Triumphantly: 'And you can see eyeball to eyeball on the telephone?' After a thoughtful pause: 'Mind you, he says there are times when a phone would come in handy – like, for instance, when he starts dealing with them American whatchercallems . . . typhoons.'

'I thought that was a kind of wind,' said Mrs Cooperman.

My mother nodded. 'Maybe they do suffer the wind, the amount they eat. According to Mendel they're all so rich in America they live on nothing else but smoked salmon and champagne and eat calves' liver three times a week.'

'Me, I prefer a nice shoulder of veal,' said Mrs Weinberg.

'With all that money you'd think they could afford a bit of bicarb for the wind,' said Mrs Kemensky.

'It's the hard boiled eggs,' said Mrs Lewis. 'That's what causes wind. When your brother gets his telephone tell him to give them a ring and say not to eat hard boiled eggs.'

'Hard boiled eggs also give terrible dreams,' said Mrs Cooperman.

'What's all this about hard boiled eggs?' my mother shouted. 'How come hard boiled eggs all of a sudden? Here I am asking about my family and all you can come out with is hard boiled eggs like some *meschuggener* chicken.'

Golda Kemensky: 'You started it, missus, with the winds.'

'Who said anything about winds?' my mother howled.

Mrs Weinberg groaned. 'Do me a favour, missus, and move. East End. West End. Southend. Just go.'

Mrs Cooperman made placatory shush-ing noises. 'As my Leonard once said, home wasn't built in a day. I know what he means because he said it when we moved here from Golders Green. It's understandable when you got such a decision to make. I know; I've had experience. To give up a nice place there for . . .' She indicated with outstretched arms . . . 'for this.' Hurriedly: 'I'm not criticizing the people, you understand. You are nice ladies. But nobody's going to pretend it's the Vale of Health, are they?' In unison the others shook their heads. 'But as Leonard says, wherever we live is our . . .' she giggled. '. . . our little love nest. Like from the birds. And a bird in West Ham is worth two in Shepherd's Bush.' She frowned. 'At . . . at least he said something like that . . . What he means is that you got to weigh the pros and cons.'

'My mother's turn to frown. 'Rosen-Cohns? From Rosens I know thousands, and Cohns I also know. There was Morrie Cohn, the tailor's presser with the phlegm (may it never happen here), and his son, Basil, who played the violin. Mind you, he played it *outside* the

Bohemian Rooms, but at least he played. But as for Rosen-Cohn, like it was some posh double name . . .' She shook her head. 'Or did you say frozen?' Suddenly angry again: 'Anyway what's with weighing? How will weighing these people solve my troubles?'

Mrs Cooperman opened her mouth, but Mrs Lewis said quickly: 'What do the children think about it? What's from their opinions?'

My mother stared at her. 'Opinions? Since when have these *schnips* of kids, these toerags, been allowed opinions about my mother? (May she live to be a hundred and twenty and never suffer so much as a cold.) Opinions yet! But since you ask, I'll tell you.' My mother extended work-scarred and arthritis-distorted fingers. 'So for fifty years, like everyone else I've cut my own nails, and cleaned them with matchsticks or corners of newspapers. But Ruth? She's from a manicurist. For cutting nails she gets paid good money already . . . So if people are mad enough, good luck to her.

'What I'm saying is that to live in the East End still means she's got to work in the West End, which is the only place people are stupid enough to pay for people to cut their nails. And that means more distance. More fares.'

Mrs Lewis scratched her head. 'But your Ruthie works local, no? And since when has Kilburn been the West End?'

‘I’m in no mood for riddles,’ my mother retorted. After a series of thoughtful nods: ‘Maybe in the West End they want them cut shorter – like so much an inch . . . So if she’s ambitious enough to want to earn extra money an inch in the West End, who are you to deny her?’

It was Mrs Kemensky’s turn to intervene with a jocular: ‘What does your Simon think? After all, he’s your son and heir.’

My mother, sourly: ‘Heir? Only the rich have heirs. All the poor have is aggravations.’ I ducked as she threw a half-peeled potato at me. ‘So talk! Say! Speak! Don’t stand there like a stuffed dummy!’

Diplomatically I ventured: ‘I don’t care where I live, Mum – as long as you’re happy.’

‘He’s a treasure,’ breathed Mrs Lewis.

‘So go bury him,’ said my mother.

My mother considered consulting Rabbi Tsimmus about the advisability of moving, but the prospect of a long, incomprehensible lecture illustrated with quotations from the Old Testament, Talmud and Cabbala, and the tractates of obscure mystics, was too much for her. Instead she asked the advice of Iron Foot Yossell Teitelbaum when we were next visited by that pedlar of bibles, prayer books, shawls, amulets and other religious accessories – his trade giving him, in my mother's view, near-rabbinic status.

Even if one didn't buy anything (and few people did), it was customary to give him a few coppers, but my mother reasoned it was less expensive to invite him in for a cup of tea. As usual, he accepted – and an hour later licked a finger to glue the remaining crumbs from a kitchen table that had groaned under the weight of brown, white and black bread; salt, pickled and chopped herrings; fried fish; jams and honey; four choices of cheese; strudel, cheesecake and biscuits; and such side dishes as radishes, spring onions and cucumber (fresh and pickled).

'A lovely appetite,' said my mother with genuine admiration. With an elaborate attempt at nonchalance: 'I wonder if you might be able to give me some advice?'

A belch, followed by a modest shrug. 'Advice? When He whose name I'm not worthy to mention gives the guidance, then I can advise. Otherwise, take the advice from Rabbi Pinkus whose Commentaries I've got handy in my suitcase. In real Yiddish, and only seven-and-six a copy. For you – six shillings. Can I say fairer than that?'

My mother gestured impatiently. 'Books! Who's got time for books, when I haven't even read last week's *Sunday Pictorial*, what with one thing and another. What I want to know is this' – and again she summarized her awful dilemma.

When she'd finished, Yossell nodded gravely and finger-combed his beard. 'It depends on God's will,' he pronounced finally.

My mother groaned. 'I thought it might be.' Seeing the puzzlement on Yossell's face: 'So what *is* His will?'

Yossell spread his hands. 'Who are we to know? To question? All we can say is that our troubles, like this war, are tests to see if we are worthy for Paradise. For the next world.'

'The next world. Death. What is it that everybody's wishing on me all of a sudden?'

Yossell made tutting sounds of disapproval. 'Who said anything about death? At least not in the way you mean. This life is merely a stepping-stone, Mrs Ashe.' He frowned. 'You do hope for a life after death, don't you?'

A hollow laugh. 'All I want is that there should be life during life.'

Again Yossell frowned. 'But you are alive.'

'You call this living?'

Yossell sucked in his cheeks and chewed at them. 'So how can I advise?' He rubbed his hands together. 'You want to cut the cards?'

My mother's eyes widened and she licked her lips. A compulsive toucher of wood and crosser of fingers, she had reverential respect for people blessed with the gift of foretelling the future from crystal balls, tea leaves or cranial bumps, who could read palms or go into trances – but above all those who were able to interpret the significance of playing cards that had been shuffled, cut into three piles and then arranged in vertical rows.

But her excitement vanished as quickly as it came. 'There are people marvellous at reading the cards – but you? Whose cards said there wouldn't be no war?' Hopefully: 'Unless them cards were worn out and perhaps you've got a new pack?'

Yossell shook his head. Solemnly: 'The same pack, Mrs Ashe, that was blessed personal by Rabbi Pinkus.'

'So how come they said there wouldn't be a war? Eh? Answer me that.'

'Who shuffled and cut the cards?' Yossell countered hotly. 'Rabbi Pinkus?'

My mother bit her trembling lower lip. 'You mean . . . You mean maybe I . . . well, cut them wrong?' A slow, whistled exhalation of breath. Then, with a terrible screech of rage: 'You mean it's my fault there's a war? Is that it? That it's all because I cut the cards wrong? How can you say such a wicked thing? You should have your mouth washed out with carbolic . . .' Triumphantly: 'And all right, suppose for the sake of argument that I did cut them wrong. So whose fault is that? Eh? Mine, or the lousy landlord?'

Yossell gaped. 'The landlord?'

'Of course the landlord. Who else but the landlord? That *vershtinkener* Harry Jaye. Him and the rotten council. They're the ones.'

'B-but how?'

'Because of the damp in this stinking sewer of a flat. That's how. Harry Jaye wouldn't do nothing. The council wouldn't do nothing, even though I went down on my bended knees. So my fingers are crippled with arthritis and I can't cut the cards proper. If there's a war, blame them. Don't dare blame me. D'you hear . . .' Silence as she calmed down, then: 'So we'll forget the cards.' With a shy smile: 'Maybe you'll have one of your feelings instead.'

'It's funny you should say that,' said Yossel quickly. 'Just as we were talking I had a feeling like I haven't had since Hitler (may his teeth grow hair) started the concentration camps. I said at the time it would be bad for the Jews, and was I wrong? And now I've got the feeling that in the pack of cards in my pocket there's the queen from hearts.'

'Meaning?'

'Think, Mrs Ashe. Think.'

'You think,' my mother retorted. 'I'll listen.'

'It means happiness, Mrs Ashe. Happiness.

My cousin's cousin on the mother's side, Betty Shapiro, had this terrible disease (may we be spared the like). I can't remember from the name, but a disease. Then one day I had this feeling of the queen from hearts, and as He whose name I'm not worthy to mention is my judge, within the week she was cured.'

'She was cured?'

'By my life. Right as rain.'

A contemptuous snort. 'So how can that have been a disease? When my Nathan (may he rest in peace), was ill, he died within the month. Now that's what I call a disease.'

'*Oi veh*,' said Iron Foot Yossell.

'I couldn't agree more,' said my mother. 'You want another cup of tea? It won't take a minute.'

TWO

Inevitably, the matter was resolved at my grandmother's home in Zanzibar Terrace – a bleak, narrow and damp row of disintegration that lay north of London Docks between Commercial Road and Cable Street. Granny Abrams lived on the three floors above Madam

Koski's Superior Corset Salon with her eldest son, Mendel, his wife, Zillah, their children, and my grandmother's youngest son, Benjamin.

While other uncles worked as tailors' cutters or pressers, cabinet makers, barbers, taxi drivers and the like, Mendel was 'the businessman. The dealer.' Interpreted, this meant that he spent his life buying extraordinary bargains – job-lot rolls of mis-patterned wallpaper; slightly-rotted rubber underpants ('so they're a bargain for people with just a small bladder trouble'); cracked magic-lantern slides and scratched gramophone records; souvenir daguerreotypes of long-forgotten rabbis; consignments of ungummed cigarette paper; fragmented leads for propelling pencils; rusted walking-stick ferrules ('so if I buy sticks, paint them white, then nail on the ferrules, the blind are going to know the difference?') – purchases which he would sell after gargantuan efforts for minuscule profits.

He was, in fact, the classic dupe, the true salesman's eternal victim. Anyone who found himself with the unsaleable on his hands homed unerringly on Uncle Mendel, while Ben earned pocket money (and a hernia) pushing barrow-loads of improbabilities to and from Zanzibar Terrace. It was true that Mendel had had something of a coup at the beginning of the First World War when half-inch elastic had been in short supply, and he'd had a near-monopoly of it in the East End; but I discovered that this was accidental: he had bought it in 1910 and it had lain decomposing in Madam Koski's basement until there was that sudden, fortuitous shortage. But it was this above all else that the family remembered.

The eternal optimist, Mendel was convinced that his next deal would be the really big one; of such staggering magnitude it would enable him to realize his supreme ambition – take us all to live in the wild luxury of New York.

If Uncle Mendel was the family genius, Uncle Ben – thin, untidy and dandruffed, with a broken nose that had set sideways, and a curious flat-footed shuffle of a walk – was its black sheep.

Granny Abrams was withering in her contempt of Ben who, under age, had joined the army in 1915 and was awarded the Military Medal at the Somme when he rescued a wounded officer under fire. He was mildly shell-shocked in the process, and this manifested itself in bizarre outbursts which I, as a child, regarded as hysterically comic. Once he was only just saved from arrest when caught running down Wentworth Street in his underwear and medals shouting 'Hang the Kaiser!' and on another occasion caused a panic at a local synagogue when he interrupted the Sabbath morning service with the cry: 'Put on your gas masks – the bastards are using phosgene!' Generally, however, he was quiet and self-contained, spending long periods staring at the dining room wallpaper and periodically attempting to pluck the tulips with which it was patterned.

My grandmother's feelings towards Ben's army service did not reflect any lack of gratitude towards the country that had given her refuge. Indeed, three other sons had served in the First World War, but as she once put it: 'To go into the army is bad enough. If they take you to the barracks what can you do? And when they want you they'll take you soon enough. But to go from your own free will – to *ask* to join – this is a sane man? . . . A disgrace! . . . And to save the life from an officer yet. Isn't it the act of a madman who wants certification? A madman. Who gives the orders to start the pogroms and kill the Jews if not the officers? So mine own son behaves like a *vershtinkener* Cossack and saves his life. For this God gave me children? . . .'

Ben wasn't at home when we arrived that Sunday, but the rest of us gathered in the dining room as the lunch cooked. Although it was barely midday, we sat in almost total darkness. Uncle Ben, having volunteered to rejoin the army, and having been turned down on the grounds of fitness and age, was now deeply involved in Air Raid Precautions, particularly the protection of 23 Zanzibar Terrace. An item of these safeguards, as urged by Government propaganda, had been to stick strips of brown paper across the window panes to minimize the danger of flying glass in the event of blast – but Ben had performed the task with such zeal that daylight was reduced to slivers of brown opacity.

'Ben done a thorough job,' said my mother, looking bleakly towards the dining room window. Cautiously: 'Maybe too thorough?'

'He's a madman,' said Mendel vehemently. 'Off his rocker.'

'He means well,' said my mother.

'Means well?' Mendel roared. 'Means well?' You know what that *dumkopf* did the other day? May God strike me dead then cripple me for life if I lie . . . Sand.'

'What's with sand?' asked my mother.

Mendel sighed. 'On the wireless they said they was distributing free sand for people to put in sacks to make sandbags. Like to pile outside buildings for protection. And Ben, my clever brother, what does he do? Takes the barrow and brings back load after load of sand.'

My mother: 'What's wrong with that?'

'Wrong? I'll tell you what's wrong. All over England there's a shortage of sacks. That's what's wrong.' He waved clenched fists above his head. 'So now I've got a cellar full of sand.'

'Well, you never know,' said my mother placably. 'Sand might always come in handy.'

Granny Abrams' false teeth positively rattled with rage. 'But before it went in the cellar you should have seen! All mine pillow cases and cushion covers he'd taken in the street to fill with sand. I caught him just as he was tying string round the legs of my best bloomers to turn them into bags for sand.'

'*Oi veh*,' said my mother, appalled. 'You should talk to him about these . . . well, things he does.'

'Talk?' My grandmother shrugged. 'Talking to him would do as much good as rubbing Sloane's Liniment on a corpse.'

My mother, tactlessly: 'A pity you didn't buy up these sacks, Mendel, before they went short.'

He stared at her, furious. Then a dismissive: 'Sacks! Who's got time to think of sacks? You got to think what they call big. It stands to reason – like Edward G. Wassisname in that picture I saw at the Gaumont.' Admiringly: 'Now there's a man who thinks big. Big? What am I saying? He's a colossal.

Do you know, so sure as I'm sitting here, he was a no one from nowhere in this little town in what they call Missy-something-or-other. Didn't have two ha'pennies to rub together – only there they call them dimes. Then this feller – the one with the moustache who was after the girl who was the waitress with the bad foot in the saloon – offers him a job as a butcher. A butcher! But Edward G thinks big – you follow? Why be a butcher cutting meat when you can grow your own? It stands to reason.

'So he sells up the house and with the money buys an ox and a cow. Which is logical when you want to grow beef, no? So the two become four, and four becomes eight – and before the picture's over at half past ten in the evening he owns half of Texas and cattle you can't even count by the million. So sure my children should marry, cattle by the million. And from what? From one lousy ox and a cow. If I lie, may my name be forgotten by God . . .' His ebullience suddenly evaporated. Morosely: 'Mind you, if I could get my hands on some sacks I could also raise the capital for a few cows.'

Granny Abrams: 'Cows? Where will you keep cows?' Helpfully: 'Maybe with all that sand downstairs you could grow camels instead? . . . But what's this talk of selling the house to raise the money for them? For one thing it's *my* house, and for another we don't own it to sell.'

Mendel waved a fist. 'In America there's these people who've only to press a button, read what they call the tickletapes, and they raise millions. Billions. So I'm not capable to pressing a button or reading a tickletape? Just one big deal – just one – and we'll all be over there, pressing and reading. You mark my words.'

'Talking of tapes and buttons reminds me of the elastic,' said my mother. 'And if tape and buttons are so valuable, maybe you got some in the cellar under all that sand. Get Ben to have a look.'

'Tape. Buttons,' said Granny Abrams wearily. 'All I know is that this talk of cows has made me hungry. Herschel, go to the kitchen and see how your mother's doing with the dinner.' As my cousin left the room, Granny Abrams quoted the Yiddish proverb: 'To the rich, God gives food; to the poor, appetites.'

'We don't go hungry,' Mendel protested.

'God be thanked.' My grandmother nodded with some vehemence. 'Not like in the old days in Poland. In them days there was people so poor that if they wasn't religious and fasted three days a week they'd have starved to death.' A few more nods then, matter-of-factly: 'You got to admit, Mendel, that what you see at the pictures don't make *lockshen* soup.'

'How have you managed these last few weeks, Mendel?' my mother asked quickly. 'I mean – no pictures.'

Even the boils on my uncle's neck seemed to swell with rage. 'What a dirty, diabolical liberty! Eh? The war breaks out and they close down the picture palaces. So how am I to know what's happening in the world? Mad, eh? The one thing you need is the pictures, and this *meschuggener* Government closes them.'

'But they're open again,' my mother pointed out. 'And it was only three weeks.'

'Only? So how do I know what happened those three weeks?'

'You could've read the papers,' said my mother.

'Papers?' Mendel shrugged away the suggestion. 'Papers I need for wrapping, not reading.'

My mother, a compulsive reader of newspapers, was clearly appalled by this near-heresy, but she managed a weak: 'What about the wireless?'

A dismissive: '*Mnyeh!* The wireless! . . . *Band Waggon*. Music. "We'll Hang Out Our Washing On The Siegfried Line".' Grudgingly:

'So OK, the nine o'clock news. But it's all talk. You don't *see* what's happening, like with the newsreels. And how can the wireless help me with my business plans? For them I need to know what's happening in America. Not listen to *It's That Man Again* . . . So I went to the manager of the Troxy and told him straight. Eyeball to eyeball, like with James Cagney in that picture with George Raft.'

My mother whistled with admiration. 'You mean . . .?'

The implication of the unfinished question was not lost on Uncle Mendel who winked, inflated his chest and finger-sharpened his moustache ends. 'All I'm saying is that the pictures are open again, and tomorrow I'm going to see that one with Robert Doughnut.'

'You should be in the Government,' my mother breathed. 'They could do with a real Yiddisher brain like yours. You, with your eyeballs, could work wonders . . . Mind you,' she added quickly, 'as long as it's nothing dangerous. You can't be too careful with eyeballs. They're very important for seeing.'

My uncle scratched his head, temporarily nonplussed. 'Yes . . . Sure . . . Eyeballs . . .' Then, grasping his jacket lapels: 'The eyeballs can wait. I got a deal going that could lead to thousands. Thousands! And you know what it is?' When nobody volunteered a guess: 'Paint. Yellow paint.'

'Really?' said my mother politely.

'This house could do with a paint,' said Granny Abrams, 'but I don't fancy yellow. It's unlucky.' She spat three times to ward off the evil eye.

'Unlucky?' Mendel bellowed. 'How can it be unlucky if it's going to bring in money? Anyway, it's not for painting. You can't paint with it. Five hundred tins – all set solid.'

My mother blinked. 'I know you're a genus, Mendel, and I don't want to question – but paint set solid? From this you'll make a fortune?'

A deafening: '*Ah-ha!* . . . Lew Moscow who I got it from also thought I was crazy. But he's the one that's crazy. And for why? I'll tell you. You know there's the danger from gassing. You, Minnie, always carry your gas mask, no?'

My mother felt for the brown carrier bag at her feet. Mine was white, Ruth's green, but their contents were identical: gas mask fortified by first aid kit – iodine and Lysol, bandages, lint and cotton wool; Thermos flasks of *lockshen*, bean or barley soup or *borsht* (according to the soup of the day); a packet of biscuits, sandwiches, safety pins and Ex-Lax. (As my mother had put it: 'If, God forbid, we get gassed, at least we won't starve, bleed or constipate to death.')

'Well,' Mendel continued, 'gas can do funny things. I saw in this picture with Boris Karloff. He was working with this other fellow – you know, the one that drinks the blood – and they're trying to find ways of making this shrinking gas. So some escapes through just this tiniest hole in the window the hunchback (*oi*, what a lunatic!) forgot to mend. You follow? So I saw with my own eyes, in black and white, what happened – and may God punish me with a black year if I lie. For the gas doesn't go like . . . like a cloud up the street and round the corner.' He stretched his fingers and waggled them. 'Some goes here, some goes there, and some goes nowhere. Now do you see? . . . You don't?' Mendel smiled. 'So I'll explain.

'In case from gas attacks the Government's been painting those yellow stripes on the pillar boxes and walls of houses. You've seen for yourselves. And for why? I got the answer personal from the Air Raid Warden at number thirty. If there's gas then this yellow paint gets blisters.'

'God keep us alive!' my mother exclaimed. 'You . . . you mean we all got to paint ourselves yellow? Otherwise we won't know from whether we're being gassed, unless we see ourselves with shrinking blisters?'

Instead of the rage I'd expected, Uncle Mendel beamed. 'You're getting close, Minnie. I always said that from among the girls in the family you was the one with brains . . . It's like this: the gas comes down. But since, like I said, it goes all over the place, how you going to be sure it lands on that bit of paint on the pillar box? Maybe it'll miss the pillar box altogether and land on somebody's front door. What then?'

'*Oi veh*,' my mother groaned.

Mendel tapped a finger against his temple. 'So this is where thinking big comes in. Everyone should have yellow paint on the door. But they don't get it. And even if they did, what's the good of one lousy lick of paint? In London, with all the filth in the air, you need undercoats, overcoats, raincoats – God knows how many coats. Otherwise it's gone in no time. So what's the answer? I'll tell you. A good thick slice of yellow paint.

'So now you see. The paint from Lew Moscow. I'll get Ben to cut away the tins, and then with a saw cut the paint into slices. All people got to do is nail a slice to the door. So from each tin I worked out fifty slices, and from five hundred tins at say a shilling a slice? . . . Eh? . . . Work it out for yourself. May God strike me deaf, dumb and blind, and then give me piles if I lie, but we're going to be on the way to a fortune. So who's the madman now, eh? Me, or Lew Moscow? Now you see what I mean by thinking big. Because as soon as I saw that paint it came to me in a flash.' He snapped his fingers. 'Like that.'

My sister ventured: 'But if the war's going to be over by Christmas, Uncle Mendel . . .?'

'Between now and Christmas there's still time to go,' he replied severely. 'And how long will it take to gas people?'

At that moment Aunt Zillah came in with the chopped liver and asked: 'Where's Ben?'

'Collecting the paint,' said Mendel.

'Let's make a start,' said my grandmother. 'Ben can have his later. Keep it warm. I'm starving.'

Five minutes later we heard the front door open and slam, followed by Uncle Ben's heavy tread on the stairs. He came into the dining room wearing what he called his battle order. On his head was a souvenir of the Somme: a battered German helmet with a spike on the top, and which he'd crudely painted with the letters ARP. His jacket was an old khaki uniform top to which his medals were pinned, while puttees were wrapped round his legs between brilliantly-polished boots and the knees of patched flannel trousers. He carried his gas mask in a haversack, and both sleeves were hidden by home-made brassards of varying colour and size which announced: ARP . . . OLD SOLDIER . . . YIDDISH SPOKEN . . . HANG HITLER . . . NO SURRENDER . . . CARELESS TALK COSTS LIVES . . . AIR RAID WARDEN . . . BLACK-OUT INSPECTOR . . . ODD JOBS DONE and GOD SAVE THE KING.

After an exchange of greetings, he took off his helmet, sat down and said: 'I got the paint.'

'I should hope so. You been long enough.'

Flatly: 'It isn't yellow.'

Slowly, from neck upwards, Mendel's face purpled. 'Wh-wh-what's that? N-Not . . .?' For some seconds he was too choked with emotion for speech. Finally: 'Y-you mean that dirty rotten shitpot, Moscow, has cheated me? Done me down?'

Ben shook his head. 'The paint *was* yellow. It said on the tins. But 'cause it's so old it's gone a sort of brown.'

'Brown!' Mendel howled. 'Brown! What d'you mean, brown? What's the good to me of brown paint? How do I sell slices of brown paint? Like it's slices of Yiddisher rye bread or something?' He raised trembling hands across the table in the general direction of Ben's throat. 'Cabbage! *Dumkopf!* Traitor! Mosleyite! . . . God help me! . . . Mother, pass that carving knife so I can tear his guts out! . . . In America they got assistants like James Stewart and Micky Rooney from Yale and what they call the Socialist Registry – but me? Me? I've got that . . . that rubbish.'

'*Sssh*,' said my mother. 'Don't aggravate yourself.'

'Aggravate myself!' Mendel squealed, near-falsetto. 'I'm aggravating myself? You mean it's me and not him that's doing the aggravating?' To Ben, in a voice controlled with difficulty to almost normal: 'So tell me, you lump, why didn't you inspect?'

'I did – down in the cellar.'

Mendel: 'In the cellar . . . How many times have I told you never to buy without inspecting first? Would Rothschild buy without first inspecting? Would Rockerfeller? Cunard? Would Ruda the fishmonger buy so much as a halibut without inspecting? But you . . .'

Ben shrugged as he chewed at a slice of bread. 'All of a sudden *I* did the buying? I thought you did the buying. Me, I'm only fit to fetch and carry.'

As Mendel opened his mouth, Granny Abrams banged at the table with a spoon. 'Enough already!' Such was the authority she commanded, the room fell silent. 'Fighting in the family. Fighting. Always fighting. You got to fight? So go fight Hitler (God forbid).' In

Yiddish: 'Like it says in Torah, anger in the home is like a worm in a fruit.' Having allowed time for this to be absorbed, she resumed in English: 'And like I said myself, yellow is unlucky.'

Mendel, bitterly: 'And brown isn't?'

I asked: 'Why is it unlucky, Granny?'

She spread her hands. 'It always has been. Today in Germany they make the Jews wear yellow badges. In the old days it was from yellow . . . What's the word?' With a finger she described a circle on the table-cloth. 'And I remember in Poland the rabbis warned against yellow because it was the colour from gold. Because . . .' After searching for words she again lapsed into Yiddish: 'It goes back to the golden calf. Gold. Yellow. That's why Jews should worship God, not gold, the colour of the heathens.'

Aunt Zillah: 'Much chance we got of worshipping gold in this household.'

My mother: 'Maybe that's why Jews don't have yellow hair . . . At least not natural yellow.'

'What about the Golds, Goldbergs and Goldsteins?' asked Herschel – for which question his father rewarded him with a blow between the shoulder blades.

My mother gasped. 'Wait a minute! Hang on! Mendel, I got from an idea.' Diffidently:

'Maybe it's not a good one, but you'll know. In a flash you'll know. Quick as an eyeball. You're the businessman, the genus . . . But . . .'

'So go on,' said Mendel, arms crossed, head lowered, brow furrowed and lips pursed as if he were a Hassidic wonder rabbi about to pass judgement on a debate to establish the precise age of God.

'Well . . . if yellow's suddenly anti-semitic all of a sudden (although I must say it's news to me), so the Jews won't want from yellow paint on the door. In which case, what's wrong with brown? I mean, with the blisters . . .' (Absently: 'For which, personal, I always use a sharp needle that's been warmed with a match – so we'd better put needles and matches in the carrier bags . . .') Addressing herself again to Mendel: 'So for these blisters – you mean to say that gas can tell one colour from another? It's really that clever? That brainy? Because if not, what I'm saying is that paint is paint, so maybe you can sell the brown to Jewish people who don't want the yellow.'

Granny Abrams: 'And for poor people don't cut too thin.'

Again Mendel frowned in thought. Then a bellow of joy. 'Of course Jewish people! There's Jews all over. East End. West End. Golder's Green. Finchley even. And out of

London – Manchester, Sheffield, and that other place.' He slapped a hand against his forehead. 'Of course gas can't tell no different. Brown. Yellow . . . I should have thought of it earlier. We'll still make a fortune.'

A cackle of a laugh from my grandmother. 'As Rabbi Pacey used to say: "The tongue's got no bones, so it flaps".'

Mendel, belligerently: 'What's that supposed to mean?'

'If you don't know, go ask Rabbi Pacey.'

'But he's dead.'

'So what you want I should do? Bring him back to life? If I could, I'd also make a fortune.'

Aunt Zillah came in with the soup.

The conversation turned from poison gas to more immediate aspects of the war: the hazards of the blackout, and how Mendel knew for a fact that local schools and swimming baths were stacked with cardboard coffins ready to receive corpses, while the trenches being built in Victoria Park were not for protection in the event of air raids, but were really lime pits for the mass disposal of those coffins when they came to be occupied.

'I told them I'd help with the barrow,' said Ben.

My mother shuddered. 'You two got nothing

else to talk about during dinner? . . . But now you mention it, where is the nearest shelter?'

'I'm getting the cellar ready,' said Ben. 'Making it stronger.'

'I wouldn't fancy that,' said my mother firmly. 'So close to the river, one little bomb and you could all be drowned alive in your beds. And not only drowned: poisoned to death from all the filth and muck people throw in rivers. I read in the *Evening Standard* only the other day of rivers packed like sardines with dead bodies.'

'That was in India,' I said.

My mother beat me over the head with a fork. 'Don't always contradict, you ungrateful toerag! India. Africa. Timbuctoo. A river is a river, no?'

My cousin Sybil: 'But Aunty Minnie, where you are – Kilburn – isn't far from the zoo, is it? Suppose that gets bombed and you have lions and tigers and hippopotamuses come visiting?'

'*Oi gevult!*' My mother crossed her arms and grasped her shoulders. 'Lions and tigers and hippo'muses yet! It isn't bad enough I got mice the size of dogs under the floorboards – now it's going to be wild animals.'

'So that's another reason for moving in here,' said my grandmother – and the debate again got under way.

When the familiar arguments had been covered a dozen or more times, my grandmother made the point: 'And with rent and rates and gas and electric and food, it'll be a money saving.'

My mother adopted what Ruth and I called her Queen of Sheba expression – an ineffective attempt at haughty indifference. 'If you're hard-up I don't want to impose. God forbid I should take the bread from your mouth to buy food for my children. Don't worry – I can go out scrubbing. If Mrs Sinclair from round the corner can do it with one leg, then why should me being crippled with arthritis stand in the way?' She was unable to maintain this attitude for long. Lightning quick, the rage came. 'Have I ever asked for a penny? You think I like taking charity? . . . May I never leave this room alive if I take so much as another farthing! You hear? So sure I should live I'll throw it out from the window! I'd rather go beg in the streets . . . Ruthie, Simey – come. We're going home to get warm clothes, then we're going out begging.'

Uncle Mendel, meanwhile, had been deep in thought. For it was certainly true that at this time we were dependent on family charity: a pound here, ten shillings there – with Uncle Mendel doing most of the giving. So after some rabbinic tugging at an imaginary beard, he pronounced: ‘All right, go begging – but move in first.’

‘With the war over by Christmas?’ my mother countered. ‘You’ve said a dozen times.’

Mendel shrugged away this sudden contradiction of attitudes. ‘So let’s be on the safe side. If my informer is wrong (and between you and me I got it from the man at the Town Hall) – but if, for the sake of argument, he’s wrong, so what’s the harm? You’re here as long as it lasts. Christmas, Passover – what difference? It stands to reason.’

‘But when the war *is* over,’ my mother persisted.

‘By then we’ll be on our way to America,’ her brother assured her.

My mother, matter-of-factly: ‘And if we’re not?’

Mendel was outraged. ‘Not? *Not*? . . .’ After he’d gulped calming air into his lungs: ‘So you’ll find another flat.’ A flash of inspiration: ‘With no mice.’

‘No mice!’ A whistle of wonder. But this was really incidental – I could tell that my mother’s mind was made up: since both my grandmother and Uncle Mendel were now in favour of our moving to the East End, the decision was made. But there were still residual questions.

'Where do we sleep? In the cellar on the sand like them Arabs?'

'We'll make room,' Uncle Mendel assured her airily.

'Where?' asked Aunt Zillah.

Granny Abrams: 'Mrs Koski's moving out.'

Uncle Mendel: 'Since when?'

Granny Abrams: 'Since next Wednesday.'

Uncle Mendel: 'Who told you?'

Granny Abrams: 'Mrs Koski. Who else?'

Uncle Mendel: 'She never told me.'

Granny Abrams: 'So me she did tell.'

Uncle Mendel: 'B-but not to tell *me*?'

Granny Abrams, placidly: 'She's going Wednesday. Closing the business here and moving from the flat in Brick Lane to be . . . What's the word? . . . Evaporated?'

'Evacuated,' said Mendel.

My mother: 'So you want me and my babies should sleep in the shop window?'

Granny Abrams: 'Look, dolly, I've lived here a long time. And you should also remember that before it was a shop it was like part from the house. A few curtains and again it's like part from the house. A big room at the front for a bedroom for you and Ruthie, the storeroom at the back for Simey. And your own lavatory in the yard. You want fairer than that?'

My mother: 'But for this there's also going

to be rent and rates to pay. So where's the saving?'

'For one thing, in aggravations,' my grandmother replied. 'When we're all here we'll know where we are. And the others in the family live in the East End already, thank God. And with food: a potato here, a bit of meat there – it's going to make such a difference in money?'

My grandmother's mention of food coincided with my mother forking a piece of gristle from her mouth. 'So who does the cooking?' she demanded, eyes flashing.

My grandmother clicked her teeth. 'You're a good cook, Minnie. The best. No one can say different.' She lowered her head and looked sideways at her daughter-in-law. 'What you think, Zillah? Share? Take turns?'

A splutter of near-mirth from my aunt. Then, sourly: 'You think I like cooking? It's such a bargain? You fancy it's a pleasure in that kitchen?' A glare at Mendel. 'With a cooker that's falling to pieces all the time, it's a wonder I don't blow myself up – on top of having to do the scrubbing and cleaning and darning. And now, with three extra to prepare for?' She flapped a hand. 'You can do the cooking, Minnie – and welcome. And the shopping. And good luck to you. Me, I'll look after the rest.'

An '*Aaaah*' of thankful relief from my mother.

'So any more questions?' asked Mendel.

'Yes,' said my mother. 'My furniture. I know it isn't all that posh these days, but it's mine.' Quickly: 'And don't dare suggest selling it. Those sticks of furniture are mine home. All I got. My poor husband (may he rest in peace) bought it with his bare hands.'

Granny Abrams: 'Some you'll need to furnish downstairs. The rest put in the cellar.'

My mother gasped. 'How can you say such a thing?' It's soaking wet down there.'

Zillah: 'From what you always say, it can't be worse than where you're living now.'

Unexpectedly, Uncle Ben spoke. 'We got them rolls of oilcloth out the back in the yard. The ones with Edward Eighth's picture on upside down. Remember, Mendel – what you was going to make a fortune from to sell for flags for his coronation to pay the tickets for America?' (His brother's expression was one of undiluted hate.) 'So I'll wrap the furniture in the oilcloth, put it on bricks to keep away the damp – not that there'll be damp when I get the place ready for a shelter – and there you are . . . *Lockshen* soup.' Seeing the bafflement on our faces: 'I'm looking forward to your *lockshen* soup, Minnie.'

'Mine you don't eat all of a sudden?' Zillah demanded.

'Enough already,' said Mendel. 'So it's settled, eh? A good idea of mine, no?'

'Almost settled,' said my mother. 'Don't be in such a hurry. It's a big decision.'

'What else is there?' asked Mendel wearily. 'It's terrible . . . If we was in America I'd ring a bell and fifty blondes with yellow hair would deal with everything. All I'd have to do is snap my fingers. Like that.' He demonstrated. 'So I can snap my fingers. You saw with your own eyes. But what good is snapping in Zanzibar Terrace? Eh? Answer me that? But in Park Avenue I'd have Myrna Loy and Zazu Pitts to . . . *Oi*, what's the good of talking? . . . So what other problems you got, Minnie?'

'Jobs for the children when we move.'

Uncle Mendel gestured impatiently. 'Let them go to the Labour Exchange. I got bigger worries.'

'But Mendel,' my mother protested, 'with you being the genus I'd've thought that with one of them snaps of the eyeballs you could've got them fixed up real nice. You – you mean you can't?'

'*Can't?*' Mendel roared. 'Who said can't? Course I can get them jobs. You'd be surprised the people I've got started. F'rinstance, you remember Simcha Levy's boy? Hymie, the one with the warts? And you remember the kids' chemical sets I got cheap? The ones that would've gone to Woolworth's only the labels on the chemicals were mixed up or missing? So I gave one to Hymie Levy for his *bar mitzvah*, and may God strike me dead and also cover me with warts if he's not now studying to be a doctor of science.'

'A doctor of what?' asked my mother.

'Like I said: science.'

'A pity.'

'How come a pity?' asked Uncle Mendel.

Because science I don't suffer from . . . At least I don't think I do. But these days you can never be sure. So maybe he'll give me a looking-over.'

'Science, *schmience*,' said Granny Abrams. 'Every day there's something new. All it needs is probably a good dose of salts . . . Let's clear the plates and have our afters.'

THREE

My mother sat quietly weeping in the kitchen at Daffodil Square. (Weeping and weary, for after a sleepless night she had been rushing from room to room and up and down the basement stairs to make certain the removal men did no further damage to our already scratched and battered furniture.) Her seat in the kitchen was now the huge and crumbling American trunk in which she had packed her most valued treasures: family photographs; our silver candlesticks and knives and forks; a hideous teapot bequeathed by a neighbour; birth, death and marriage certificates; prayer books; her best corset; a plait of Ruth's hair; and a Huntley & Palmer biscuit tin in which, carefully wrapped in my father's prayer shawl, were two gramophone records I had bought to replace earlier breakages: Al Jolson singing 'Sonny Boy', and Sophie Tucker singing 'My Yiddisher Momma'.

The trunk was not to be handled by strangers. Nor was her bed ('I don't want no strange men touching the private parts where I sleep'); nor her *perrener* – a sort of white linen pillow case vast enough to cover her bed, and packed two feet thick with goose feathers. One of four that my grandparents had somehow brought with them from Poland, its immensity was now wrapped in newspapers and tied with odds and ends of knotted string.

Trunk, bed and *perrener* were not to be entrusted to the removal van, even though my mother was travelling in the van 'to keep an eye on things'. Instead, I was to help Ben push them across London on his barrow.

One other item remained in the kitchen: a coal shovel. Ruth had gone on ahead by bus carrying a cardboard box containing Itchky, our aged tabby, and my mother was convinced that the moment the door closed behind them we would be invaded by hunger-crazed mice the size of Alsatian dogs. So I had been detailed to periodically tour the flat and beat loudly on the floorboards with the shovel to keep the beasts at bay.

It was still very early, for my mother was fearful that if we did not leave at the crack of dawn we might receive an unexpected visit from the landlord, butcher, rates officer – or some other creditor anxious for a little money on account. Not that my mother was happy about avoiding them: on the contrary, her conscience bothered her – but she did not have the money, and so suffered dreadful visions of being caught in the act of moving . . . the police being called . . . our belongings seized . . . and the three of us being sent to the workhouse. ('If it was a workhouse near Mother it wouldn't be so bad, but with my luck it'll probably be the other end of Kingdom-come, like Putney or Willesden. So we'll make an early start.')

Consequently, farewells to her friends in the square had taken place the night before – long, loud and tearful, accompanied by the consumption of massive quantities of barley soup, fried plaice, cold salt beef, *lockshen* pudding and *strudel*. When the final promises to keep in touch, pledges of everlasting friendship, and assurances of happy memories had been made, it was past midnight.

Now my mother sat slumped on the American trunk and wept over fragmented recall of twenty years in Daffodil Square that had begun after her honeymoon at Westcliff-on-Sea . . .' And even them tradesmen weren't so bad to us . . .' She listed names, nodding in generous forgiveness – until she realized she'd mentioned Sam Mendoza, the butcher. She sat erect and gasped. 'What am I saying? I must be potty. Mendoza, that . . . that thief! I must be going soft in the head.' The enormity of her error brought an immediate end to sentimental reminiscence. 'Simon – go bang on the floors. And what's keeping Ben? We've got to make a move.'

My uncle arrived soon afterwards, at about seven-thirty. After the formality of asking after his health, my grandmother's health, Mendel's health, Zillah's health, and the health of my cousins, my mother said: 'You'll have a bowl of soup.'

'This time of the morning?'

'So for soup there's a time?'

'But I just had breakfast.'

'There's always room for a drop soup. I got hot in my Thermos. Made special. Seven pounds of bones went into that soup. Strong like iron. We had last night. It's really nice, if I say so myself.'

'Not just now, thanks all the same.'

'So what's the matter with my soup all of a sudden? You used to like it.'

'I still do. But—'

'No buts. But my life you'll have a drop. A mouthful. So sure I should live you won't leave until you've at least tasted it. After all, you got a long way to push, all the way to the East End. You need the strength. And this builds blood.'

Ben nodded. 'We got the time?'

'There's always time for a drop soup.'

'With the landlord due any minute?' Ben

clenched his fists and adopted a fighting pose. 'Mind you, if he does come I could always smash in his face for him, eh?' He demonstrated with the *perrener*. 'Bang! Bang!'

My mother screamed with horror. 'OK, maybe you're right. There's no time for soup. But what you will take is a packet sandwiches and cake. I got ready in the hall. Have them on the way. It's a long time before we have dinner, and I read in the paper only the other day that it's very dangerous to eat on an empty stomach.'

After I'd helped Ben load his barrow, we made our departure from Daffodil Square. It was daylight now, and no unexpected visitor (nor other residents) could have failed to see the van with REMOVALS on its side, Uncle Ben's barrow, or my mother's cronies gathered around the gate to the basement – but the women made their final farewells in exaggerated mime: a finger against pursed lips followed by winks, waves, the blowing of kisses and the dabbing of handkerchiefs against eyes.

With enormous dignity, my mother allowed herself to be assisted into the back of the van, the tailboard was locked into place, and from the depths of an armchair behind it an arm became visible as she made regal gestures with her umbrella.

Having seen the van move round the corner, Ben said: ‘Let’s go.’

We went – and I was also sad to be leaving Daffodil Square: I had spent the first fifteen years of my life there and I too had memories . . .

It did not take my mother long to settle down in Zanzibar Terrace. Beneath all else was that abstract my grandmother called ‘being together in time of trouble’; one way of describing the imprint on the collective consciousness of persecution, ghettos, pales of settlement and religious observance which resolved into the precept that safety from danger lay in the communal womb of family.

So my mother soon adjusted, made the acquaintance of new neighbours, and became a familiar figure among them – a short, plump, large-eyed woman of about fifty, with untidy grey hair and red cheeks, invariably dressed in bedroom slippers and a flowered apron over a black dress.

She was saddened that she didn’t have a kitchen of her own to which she could invite her friends for an eight-course ‘cup of tea’, but since the autumn of ’39 was singularly mild, she organized picnics: great spreads of food on newspaper-covered orange boxes on the pavement outside the house. Theoretically, everyone was supposed to contribute, but my mother was the largest donor since she was contemptuous of anyone else's cooking (even a meagrely-buttered slice of bread or an over-cooked potato pancake were crimes for which flogging with red-hot pokers should have been the most charitable of punishments). Yet she was not sorry when rationing limited their gatherings to talk and domestic tasks (sewing, knitting, darning, the preparation of vegetables) for her picnics soon became, over a widening radius, magnets for the underfed whom she didn't have the heart to refuse a piece of cake, a middle cut of fried plaice, a salt-beef sandwich or a bowl of soup – generosities of which Uncle Mendel approved in theory, but not in terms of replacements to the household larder.

Inevitably, my mother's new cronies were almost entirely from the ranks of the street's widows – she was never able to overcome a certain resentment towards women, apart from those in the family, who had husbands living.

There was Bessie Klopps, with pot-scourer grey hair and wrinkled leather skin, whose husband had been an assistant caretaker at the Fieldgate Street Great Synagogue, and so was the group's authority on religious matters.

Mrs Block (nobody seemed to know her

first name) was the eldest of them: a morose woman whose husband, a butcher, had died of some unspecified 'condition' – which, because of his trade, my mother took to mean that the authorities had finally caught up with him and he'd been hanged. She was also convinced, again because of Hymie Block's trade, that beneath his widow's floorboards and mattress lay vast quantities of diamonds, rubies and gold. My mother never accepted Mrs Block as a real friend, but there was a hypnotic fascination in knowing (albeit by proxy) a butcher who'd actually died – and apparently in no little agony.

Another of the group was Ada Krenk. She was about my mother's age, an angular little woman and an honorary widow in that her husband, an Army corporal, had been reported missing at Passchendaele. She had interpreted 'missing' to mean 'mislaid', and since 1917 had conducted a one-sided correspondence with the King, Prime Minister, Chief Rabbi, Commissioner of Police, Editor of the *Jewish Chronicle*, Mayor of Stepney and others, demanding that if they'd mislaid Moishe Krenk it was their duty to find him. ('Quite right,' said my mother. 'For what else do we owe rates?')

Mrs Krenk was furious never to have received a reply to her postcards, but the absence of even a formal acknowledgement was made apparent (in some part at least) when I was entrusted to take a pile of post-cards to the pillar-box at the corner of Zanzibar Terrace and saw that all were lacking both postage stamps and the name and address of sender. (By this time, she was not only asking about her husband, but was denouncing various people in the neighbourhood as anti-semitic spies in the pay of the Germans.) Not that it was easy to read the cards, even though they were written in capital letters – she started with bold lettering, then, as she seemed to realize that the card would not contain all her message, the lettering grew smaller and smaller until the last lines over-lapped . . . and overlapped . . . and overlapped.

My mother was awed that Mrs Krenk dared write to such distinguished people. Even if, as I explained to her, any sort of reply was impossible, she still had a near-deferential respect for someone with the nerve to write to the King of England, the Prime Minister, the Chief Rabbi, the Editor of the *Jewish Chronicle* and the Commissioner of Police. (The Mayor of Stepney she discounted: it was rumoured that 'in real life' he was a draper.) When she came to ask Mrs Krenk why she didn't put stamps or her name and address on the cards, Mrs Krenk was at first furious that my mother should be in possession of such confidential details, then explained: 'Who can afford stamps? And my name and address I used to put on. Regular. So they know by now. In any case, I need the space to express my feelings.'

Mrs Krenk was very chummy with Uncle Ben who found her a tireless audience for his tales of life in the trenches during the Great War, and there was much heavy humour from Uncle Mendel on the possibility of Ben marrying her, and that with a bit of luck she'd get him mislaid, too.

The exception to the widows-only rule was Rosie Speck, an enormously fat dressmaker in her forties with peroxided hair and a squint, who was accepted because she'd never had a husband. Not that there had been lack of opportunities: she had endless reminiscences of ardent wooing by taxi drivers, bakers, stall holders in Petticoat Lane, tailors and bookmakers' runners; even the son of a grocer in Wentworth Street who had branches in Bow Road and Spitalfields Market. Most impressive of all – an optician. 'Well, perhaps not an actual optician, if you see what I mean, but he made the cards for them eye tests. Hand made in Yiddish. So he was more important than the optician, if you see what I mean, because without the cards how could the optician have made the glasses? All the Yiddisher people in

England would have been blind, if you see what I mean.'

It was the optician who had taken her to the West End where he'd pledged eternal love over Vienna sausages at Bloom's of Berwick Street, 'with Eddie Cantor in person at the next table'. But in the end she discovered that he couldn't dance – 'Not even the Lambeth Walk, if you see what I mean' – so that was that. Other romances had had similarly tragic endings, and while her companions on the Zanzibar Terrace pavement were suitably moved by these heart-breaking accounts of unrequited love, Ruth confided to me that many of their basic plots were localized adaptations of stories she herself had read in *The Oracle* and *Red Letter*.

But Rosie Speck hadn't given up hope, and from time to time hinted at 'A nice fellow, if you see what I mean' she'd met at a function at the Cottage Grove or La Boheme or some other ballroom. To keep herself attractive, she not only bleached her hair, but used lipstick and rouge. Then came the day when my mother said: 'Did you know that to dye your hair yellow is unlucky?'

'So far I haven't had much luck,' Rosie Speck agreed. 'I was thinking of changing anyway, if you see what I mean. What colour you fancy would suit? I read that red's getting fashionable.'

From my mother, a doubtful: 'Really? I didn't see that, and I read the papers cover to cover.'

'It was in *Peg's Paper*.'

'That I don't read,' my mother admitted.

Mrs Block: 'Go red and people will shout "Ginger you're barmy".'

Miss Speck: 'Not ginger. Red.'

Mrs Block: 'There's a difference?'

My mother: 'And ginger's a sort of yellow, and so also unlucky.'

Mrs Krenk: 'So you said before. So say – why is it unlucky?'

'My mother said. She knows. From the old country. The golden calf.' She giggled. 'Mind you, these days calves' liver costs like gold.' Pointedly: 'But your husband being a butcher, Mrs Block, you'd know, eh? With the money he left you probably eat from it every day.'

The butcher's widow uttered a hollow laugh. 'Chance would be a fine thing. My Hymie (may he be sitting at God's left side) worked for Solly Kugel who had the shop in Floral Street. For all I know, Kugel eats calves' liver for breakfast. But Hymie? He was a hand at a couple pounds a week.'

'But he must have got a few bits and pieces free,' my mother insisted. 'How can you say otherwise? A hand with Kugel. A foot. An arm. What difference? Whoever heard of a hungry butcher, eh girls?'

The others nodded their agreement.

'Have it your way,' said Mrs Block flatly. 'Just say why yellow is unlucky.'

'My Moishe had a gold-coloured badge on his cap before they mislaid him,' said Mrs Krenk. 'So maybe Mrs Ashe has got a point.'

'And I got a gold ring on mine finger,' said Mrs Klopps.

Rosie Speck screamed. 'Is that why you're . . . you're all widows? . . . Believe me, if anyone offers me a gold ring I'll throw it in his face.' She paled as the enormity of the threat sank in. 'Well . . . Anyway . . . I'll ask for platignum, if you see what I mean.'

It was my mother's turn to scream. '*Mendel!*'

Mrs Klopps: 'What's with him? He turned yellow? He found some gold bars in that cellar of his?'

'N-no,' my mother gasped. 'But America. It's called in Yiddish the *Goldeneh Medina*, no? The Golden Land. Mendel says so himself. So if . . .' She could not bring herself to work the thought through . . . Another scream. 'And I was talking to Nathan only the other week about the Golden Book!' Further words dissolved into a ten-syllabled groan.

'Bad luck,' said Mrs Block contemptuously.

'If it's gold that brings misfortunes, where do mine come from?'

'Look under the mattress,' said my mother darkly.

Mrs Klopps: 'Gold unlucky?' A pause, then a mighty '*A-ha!* . . . At Passover, when you eat the hard boiled eggs in salt water, you put on ginger. So you're saying God wants us to pour bad luck on the eggs? And also – what colour is the middle of the eggs if not gold?'

My mother: 'Mrs Cooperman from Daffodil Square always said hard boiled eggs cause dreams. And the wind . . . And anyway, why shouldn't the ginger on the eggs be unlucky? The Jews have such good years between Passovers?'

Rosie Speck: 'Gold! Yellow! Ginger! Just tell me – what colour do I go?'

Mrs Krenk: 'Why go any colour?'

My mother: 'That's right. What's wrong with natural? Why not stick to the truth?'

'Believe me, ladies,' said Rosie Speck miserably, 'with yellow hair and a bit of make-up I go out with a fellow from time to time; but if I went back to natural you'd know what they mean in Yiddish when they say truth leads a lonely life.'

Fidgeting embarrassment, until my mother brought things back to normal with the question: 'Any of you girls like a nice slice of brown paint? My brother's going to make a fortune from it (please God), but for you I can get wholesale.'

My mother found shopping in the East End a delight, for its large Jewish population meant an enormously wide choice of Jewish tradesmen, amongst whom she soon made her presence felt as she went from dark little shop to market stall, inspecting, feeling, poking, sniffing and criticizing the produce – and insulting the men and women who dared offer it for sale. Every Friday morning Mendel gave her money for the next week's shopping, its amount dependent upon the state of business, but always with the injunction that she must keep within its limits.

'You got to work out what they call a budget,' he explained. 'With a pencil and paper write down how much you spend and what you got left.' Tucking his thumbs into the top pockets of his waistcoat: 'It's the same as running a business. Like they say: take care of the pennies and the pounds will also take care . . .' He frowned, then shrugged. 'OK, so far I'm still left with the pennies – but the pounds'll come. It stands to reason. How else did Joe Lyons start if not from one lousy rock cake?'

Granny Abrams: 'I don't know from cakes, but years ago, when we was in the wet fish, there was a Lyons couldn't speak a word from English. Was previous Lefkowitz from Czestochowa . . . Lyons in rock cakes?' She shook her head. 'One I remember was in the gowns, but—'

Mendel interrupted with a shouted: 'Do me a favour! I'm talking of one of the biggest firms in the world, and you're here with Lyons in the gowns.'

'Don't get in such a state,' said his mother. 'Don't you always say you got to make a start from nowhere? So why not from the gowns?'

Mendel ignored this. 'So like I was saying, Minnie – write down.'

My mother screwed up her face in puzzlement. 'You mean every time I buy a potato I got to put down the carrier bag, take out a pencil and paper, put on my glasses, write down – and then take off my glasses, put away the pencil and paper and . . .' She nodded thoughtfully. 'And then the same thing for a herring, for bread, for fish, for . . .' More nods. 'So just tell me one thing: by the time I've finished – if I ever finish – when am I supposed to do the cooking? Dinner you'll get to eat at tea-time, and supper you'll be lucky to have for breakfast.'

Mendel, defensively: 'You got to be businesslike. Mind you, in America they got machines for such things.'

My grandmother whistled. 'Machines yet! Maybe you can get cheap second-hand from this Lyons.'

'I haven't got enough to *shlep* without machines?' my mother demanded. 'Look Mendel, I don't like to question, but if today I got three pounds in my purse, and tomorrow two pounds, I need a machine to tell me I've spent a pound?' Her voice rose. 'You think I'm a stuffed monkey or something?'

'Now, now,' said Mendel soothingly. 'You do what you think best. Me – I've got bigger things to worry about.' He flicked at his moustache-ends.

'Like with the rates?' asked Granny Abrams.

'Like with tissue paper,' her son retorted. 'In the blackout people use torches, no? And believe me, Mother, you don't go out at night, but you need them with all the rubbish in the streets these days – other people, pipes along the gutters to run water to them special tanks for the fire brigade, shelters all over the place, motor cars with hardly no lights, sandbags round everything. Mind you, if you want my opinion, there haven't been no bombs on London (God be thanked) but everywhere there's people with broken legs, so it's ARP who's doing the damage, not Hitler (may his piles turn to solid iron).

'So anyhow, the Government was worried

about them torches. Because if by accident they flash up into the sky, a German airplane can see from hundred of miles away. May God blind me for life and then give me cataracts if I lie, but so sure I'm sitting here I saw this picture from the Ministry the other day – just five minutes long but with Robert Doughnuts who was also Mr Chips – about this woman who lit a cigarette in the garden. Not even a big cigarette – a De Reszke Minor, I saw the packet – and from all them miles away a dirty rotten German bomber saw the light and down come a bomb and blew her to smithereens. Plus also the husband, four children and the girl from next door who was visiting because her father was in the Army and her mother was at the hospital giving blood.'

'I read in the papers, and I didn't like it,' said my mother firmly.

'She didn't like it either,' said Uncle Mendel hotly. 'It stands to reason – to be blown to Timbuctoo is no bargain. Believe me, I saw with my own eyes, in black and white – not read in the papers.'

'I'm talking about them blood donators,' said my mother. 'God forbid we get bombed and need blood, if it comes from one of them bottles. I mean, whose blood you going to get? What rubbish they got in them bottles? Who's to know? Eh? You thought about it?' She shuddered. 'What sort of toerags and people with God-knows-what diseases? So if I need blood, with my luck what will I get? Blood full of cholera or consumption or from some anti-semitic stinkpot, or some Ching-Chong-Chinaman from East India Dock Road. Or . . .' Another shudder. 'I don't even want to think about it . . . Anyway, Mendel, you know the man from the Town Hall, so you tell him straight: if we get bombed to death none of us want none of that yellow blood. It's unlucky, eh Mother? We want Kosher. And who's to know what was in them bottles previous? . . . In any case, you don't need donators, but soup. What's better for building blood than a good plate *lockshen* soup? Or barley soup made from all bones? You tell them, Mendel. You got influence. Tell them to ask for soup donators. Believe me, I'll be only too happy to oblige. They'll listen to you . . . Or maybe I'll get Mrs Krenk write a postcard.'

Uncle Mendel and Granny Abrams both stared at her. Finally Uncle Mendel said: 'Blood . . . Soup . . . Chinamen . . . Sure, Minnie, I'll have a word . . . In the meantime I'm talking about tissue paper.'

'So talk,' said my mother generously.

'Like I was saying: them torches. The light can be seen from hundreds of miles. So the Government want people to what they call dim them by putting tissue paper inside the glass. But there's a shortage from tissue paper.'

My mother: 'So?'

'So Schmitt, the caterer – you remember? The one Aaron had the trouble with at Vernon's wedding? When Aaron said the *schnitzels* wasn't veal, but pork?'

'Remember?' My mother's shrug swallowed her neck. 'Am I ever likely to forget? Wasn't I ill for a month?' 'Course they was pork.'

'How would you know?' I asked.

My mother took a paper chrysanthemum from the vase on the table and beat me about the head and shoulders with it. 'Don't interrupt, dogs-body!'

'I only asked.'

'Asked what?'

'How you'd know it was pork?'

'You mean all these years I've cooked and don't know meat from pork?'

'But when have you tasted pork before to compare?' I persisted.

This time she made as though to beat me with the vase itself – until Uncle Mendel restrained her. 'Pork!' she screamed. 'You saying I been feeding you pork? Mother! Mendel! You're witnesses! Eyeball to eyeball, in black and white! . . . Pork! You should have your tongue cut out and rinsed in Lysol for suggesting such a thing. To your own mother.

Pork! You should be ashamed. Should go on your bended knees and beg forgiveness. If only your father—'

'I only asked—'

'I know what you asked. And if you want an answer, it's this: that I know real veal. And if veal isn't veal – and it wasn't at Vernon's wedding – then what else was it? Lamb I also know. And beef. So if it was none of them, what was it if not pork, eh clever Dick? Answer me that . . . Mind you it serves Aaron right.' After a grunt of a verbal question-mark from Mendel: 'For weddings you always serve quarters roast chicken. That's why . . . But why's them pork *schnitzels* got to do with tissue paper? . . . Except,' she added thoughtfully, 'they was as thin as tissue paper.'

'I'll never get this story finished,' Mendel groaned. After half-a-dozen stabs at the tablecloth with a finger-end: 'Do you know, so sure I should have a good year, in the time we been sitting here discussing, Edward Arnold would have bought half New York and a quarter Chicago. And me? I can't even get as far as the lousy doilies.'

Granny Abrams: 'What's with doilies? I thought it was from Schmitt's tissue paper – only there isn't none.'

'Exactly! There isn't no tissue paper, but Schmitt had these doilies printed. Only the printer got the name wrong. You follow?' When my mother and Granny Abrams shook their heads, he ground his teeth, looked pointedly at me, then at them and said: 'Schmitt. A misprint.' He winked at them. 'You get me? Schmitt . . .' His mouth went fish-like as it silently formed an *M*. 'So can he have doilies telling his customers that if they want the best, nothing tastes like misprinted Schmitt?

'He was going to throw away five thousand doilies, but I saw in a flash.' He snapped his fingers. 'Quick like that. So I bought the lot. For if there's not tissue paper, why not them doilies cut in circles? In the blackout, who's going to read? Is it logic? Does it stand to reason?' He rubbed his hands together. 'We'll make a fortune. You mark my words.'

My mother cocked her head to one side and smiled at him. 'Maybe you could spare a few of them doilies?'

Mendel, suspiciously: 'What do we need for?'

'Not us: me. I'll fold careful so no one sees the name and use them for lists. I mean, I could use the back of envelopes, but since when did I last get a letter from anyone? And perhaps a bit of pencil you could also lend me?'

Uncle Mendel uttered a sort of growl and

flapped a hand. 'You work it out the way you want, so long you keep to the budget.'

As Granny Abrams absently picked up a fallen hairpin from the tablecloth and used the rounded end to de-wax an ear. 'What's with this budget Minnie's got to keep to when she goes shopping?'

An '*Aaaach!*' of exasperation from Mendel. 'It means we got to keep to our income.'

My grandmother's false teeth rattled castanet-like at the shock of this statement. 'Things are *that* bad?'

'Be patient,' said Uncle Mendel ominously. 'Be patient.'

It took more than an injunction from Uncle Mendel for my mother to abandon the habits of the years. The money in her purse invariably ran out by mid-week – how could she deny her mother a bit of smoked salmon, or Mendel a Dover sole, or Ben a slice of liver since she had it on good authority that it was good for hernias? Even Aunt Zillah was entitled to her favourite halibut in egg and lemon sauce . . .

So the residents of 23 Zanzibar Terrace ate more lavishly than they'd done for years – and the debts accumulated, albeit without Uncle Mendel's immediate knowledge, for the number of Jewish traders meant that these debts could be spread thinly (and widely) over the area.

There were certain shopkeepers whom my mother came to prefer to others for particular items, such as Sontag the butcher, who had a gloomily shuttered shop off Wentworth Street and when barley soup was on the menu was favoured for his generosity with free marrow bones.

I was with my mother one afternoon when she went to Sontag, asked for some chuck steak 'and a few bones – say six, seven pounds'; demanded she be allowed to see the newspapers in which they were to be wrapped in order to select journals she'd not read, and added with some reluctance: 'I haven't got the strength to drag all over London, so I'll take a chance and have a boiling fowl – if it smells good.' Satisfied (just) on this point, she made further purchases. 'So how much it come to?'

Morrie Sontag, a grey-faced little hunchback, took a stub of pencil from behind an ear and wrote figures on a scrap of greaseproof paper. 'Twenty-five shillings, Mrs Ashe.'

'Twenty-five shillings? You must be joking!'

'I haven't made a joke since my mother-in-law broke her leg and I said it could be worse and the gangrene set in.'

'What a shocking thing,' said my mother, near-sympathetic. Practically: 'Here, let's see.' She grabbed the greaseproof paper. 'You got to be patient: mine budget.' She made an elaborate show of searching for her glasses, putting them on, taking his pencil, licking its end and whispering the figures to herself as she checked his arithmetic. Morrie Sontag went on to serve another customer – and both gasped with fright when my mother uttered a shrill screech of rage.

'You – you had a bad turn?' asked the other customer.

'Turn?' my mother cried, waving the paper. 'Turn? If you worked out what I worked out, you'd have more than a turn. St Vitus Dance you'd have.' She now waved the paper under Sontag's nose. 'I know butchers are thieves. Murderers. I know you put a thumb on the scales the minute you think my back is turned. I know you should be buried alive in the earth.' To the other customer: 'You must also know, eh missus?' Back to Sontag: 'B-but barefaced robbery? Is this what the world's coming to? May God give me a black year if I don't tell my brother the businessman to report you to the Town Hall.' Again to the customer: 'You're my witness. If my poor husband was alive . . . So give my baby here your name and address . . .' But the woman fled.

'What have I done?' Morrie Sontag pleaded.

'Done? *Done?* Robbed me left, right and centre, that's what you've done.'

'How?'

'How? I'll tell you how. What I bought comes to seventeen-and-six. Not twenty-five shillings. That's how. So put that in your pipe and smoke it.'

Mr Sontag scratched his chin. 'You owed seven-and-six from last week.'

My mother paled. A deflated '*Oi veh*' . . . Cheerfully: 'So OK – now I owe twenty-five shillings.'

This time an '*oi veh*' from Morrie Sontag, followed by: 'When you going to settle up?'

A characteristic shrug. 'I'm a poor woman. A widow. With arthritis, with aggravations – and if that wasn't enough I'm now also suffering with a budget.'

'That's an illness?'

'It's nothing to dance in the streets about,' my mother retorted. 'So what do you want of my life: blood? If so, go to the Town Hall. Them Chinese is donating free.'

Mr Sontag shook his head as though to unscramble his brain. 'I don't know about blood, nor from Chinamen. All I know is you owe twenty-five shillings.'

My mother attempted an ingratiating smile. 'I'm a poor woman.'

'And if I keep giving credit all the time I'll

be worse than poor,' Sontag retorted. 'I'll go bust.'

My mother beamed at him. 'So then you also can get credit.'

With two hands Sontag picked up a knife from the counter, pointed it towards his neck, closed his eyes and muttered: 'God give me the strength to cut my throat' . . . After some seconds he flung down the knife, opened his eyes and said bitterly: 'There are times I wish I had the courage.'

'Force yourself,' said my mother – and swept from the shop.

That night Uncle Mendel arrived home in a dreadful rage, having had a glass of Russian tea at Berman's Restaurant where the butcher had also been a customer. 'What's this about owing money to Hunchback Morrie?' he demanded.

'Hunchback Morrie?'

'Sontag. Hunchback Morrie Sontag.'

'The butcher?'

'How many other Hunchback Morrie Sontags you know?'

My mother acknowledged this with an apologetic grimace. 'I bought one or two things. You, Mendel, fancied a middle fried plaice Monday. Remember?' Generously: 'Not that I begrudge. After all, it's your money. But if I done wrong, don't blame me – blame the budgets. Because before budgets owing the butcher was the natural thing to do. So if now it isn't, whose fault if not the budget? Get rid of the budgets and it'll again be the natural thing. Like you yourself would say, it's logic. It stands to reason. You follow?'

'No,' said Uncle Mendel.

'Budgets, *schmudgets*,' said my grandmother. 'For hundreds of years Yiddisher people have owed the butcher. Now there's budgets – which is what, anyway? Some Government law against the Jews? I thought they was on our side for once.'

'I'm glad you're speaking up for me,' said my mother gratefully.

Mendel clenched his fists and beat a tattoo on his skull.

'You all right, Mendel?' asked my mother, alarmed.

'No I'm not,' Mendel retorted, massaging his head. 'And I won't be all right until you stop owing the butcher.'

A shrug of acceptance. Then, hopefully: 'What about the fishmonger?'

Mendel covered his face with his hands and sobbed.

FOUR

One of the major decisions that had to be taken after our move to the East End concerned the matter of jobs. My cousin, Herschel, denied the opportunity of becoming a doctor since Uncle Mendel, despite my grandmother's pleadings, could not persuade Dr Lee to take him on as an apprentice, was working at a local bakery; Sybil served behind the counter of a draper's in Aldgate High Street.

Ruth was keen to continue as a manicurist, and the distance from Kilburn renewed her hopes of working in the West End.

'I can't understand this madness for cutting people's nails,' said Granny Abrams. 'If they was crippled, so all right – you do a good turn. But otherwise?'

'Not everyone does the dirty work,' my sister replied with an attempt at haughtiness. 'Some people are posh. So why shouldn't I also want to be genteel?'

My mother screamed and beat her savagely about the head with her fists. 'Filth! Animal!

Slut! . . . You heard, Mother, in black and white. You're a witness. And you, Mendel! So don't stand there, do something. My hands are killing me.'

'What about my head?' Ruth howled as she protected it with her hands.

'Your head?' my mother shrilled. 'It should be cut off and boiled in carbolic! Fumigated! To want to become a conversion. A Christian. God protect us.' Pausing only to spit three times to ward off the evil eye: 'A Christian in the family yet! If your poor father was alive to see it he'd turn in his grave. You should be ashamed. And in front of your own grandmother.'

I said: 'But Mum, Ruth didn't say gentile, but genteel.'

An anguished wail. 'So now my own son takes her side . . . A monster, a Finkelstein I gave birth to.' As she turned towards me, Mendel put a restraining hand round her shoulders. 'Now you're on their sides instead of standing up for me,' she screamed at him. Her rage dissolved into shoulder-slumped sobbing. 'There's no one to take my part.' As the tears rolled down her cheeks she demanded of the ceiling: 'So can't *You* do something? They used to say that God hears the prayers of the poor before anyone else's. So from me You've heard a million times already. And what happens? My daughter (may she have a black year) wants to become a Christian, and mine son and brother take her side. So You gone deaf or something? What You got against me? Just say. Tell . . .'

When no Jehovistic thunder came, my mother half-fell into a chair. Finally Granny Abrams spat three times and said: 'Christians . . . Ruthie, tell me. You really want to become a Christian?'

Ruth, fingering her skull as though testing its intactness: 'I didn't say I wanted to become a Christian. A gentile. I said genteel. G-e-n-t-e-e-l.'

'I can't read from English,' said Granny Abrams. 'I can't hardly speak. So from to spell? If you got to spell, spell Yiddish. Otherwise, just explain.'

Ruth sighed. 'Genteel means . . . well posh. Is there anything wrong wanting to be posh?'

'Posh also means gentle?' my mother asked, her voice dangerously subdued. When Ruth, tired from argument, nodded, my mother uttered a triumphant 'Ah-hah! Isn't that what I said all along? That posh people is gentles? And which of them isn't, all of a sudden? The King from England? The Duchess from York? They're not Christians? They suddenly become Jewish?'

'What's the use of arguing?' said Ruth wearily.

'No use,' replied my mother firmly. 'First thing tomorrow morning you give notice. No more with the nails. No more with the gentles.'

Ruth pouted. 'But if I get a job in the West End, Mayfair maybe, you meet very posh – I mean classy – customers. I heard only the other day of a girl who manicured the nails of a rich millionaire . . . I think he was a Rothschild,' she added quickly. Dreamily: 'And from just the touch of her fingers, and looking in each other's eyeballs – I mean eyes – True Love Triumphed.'

An *aieeee* of astonishment from my mother. 'A Rothschild? Never! . . . Anyway, you shouldn't be thinking of such things at your age.' Thoughtfully: 'Mind you, a real Rothschild could be different. After all, like Iron Foot Yossell used to say, circumcisions alter cases.'

'Faces?' asked Aunt Zillah.

'I said cases.'

'Ah . . . Because faces it don't alter,' said Zillah. 'Like from Fat Izzy in Floral Street. He says he's Jewish, but he's got a face like Edward Seven.'

'Maybe he was also a Yiddisher fellow,' said Granny Abrams. 'Changed his name. Like before he was Seven he was Sieben, which is like from Seven in Yiddish . . . Anyway, you got to go to the West End to find a Rothschild? With so many people in the East End there isn't maybe one living local? Or in one of them big houses in Dalston? I'm told they even got gardens. What you say, Mendel?'

Mendel turned to Ruth and said quickly: 'You never told me you saw that picture.'

Ruth: 'What picture? Fat chance I've got of going to the pictures, what with your doilies.' (Which was true in that Ruth, myself and our cousins were forced to spend every evening pencilling the outlines of pennies, shoe polish tins and wine-glass rims on Uncle Mendel's doilies, then cut out the discs and tie them with cotton into assorted packs of twenty; the operation urged on by my mother's curses and blows, and warnings not to disgrace Uncle Mendel.)

Mendel ignored this. 'What you heard, Ruthie, about the manicure girl was almost the same as in real life from Joan Crawford at the Gaumont in that picture with the one who's also sometimes a cowboy. Only it wasn't Mayfair, but America. That place in New York: Cohen Island . . . so you're right about being Jewish. And the way that girl lived! Oi, her apartment – which is what they call a flat over there. Such rooms! Such furniture! Not a speck of dust, and all the time music playing. No matter where she was – at work, on the bus (except she only travelled by car or taxi), even when she was in the bathroom (and so sure I should live she had a bathroom – a manicurist with a bathroom, eh?) – music. With a choir . . . So where was I? . . . Ah yes, so this fellow who's a millionaire from the Socialist Registry, goes four times a week to get his nails cut, and—'

'Four times a week?' my mother interjected. 'His nails must've been down to the knuckles. Painful.'

'What Uncle Mendel means,' said Ruth with a smirk, 'is that being a posh – swank – manicurist is a good job to have. Bathrooms. Music. Taxis. Millionaires. What can be bad about that?'

My mother glared at Mendel. 'So again you take her side?' she demanded. 'Is that it? You're also against me. You, my own brother. The family genus.'

Mendel inflated his chest and twirled his moustache-ends. 'America is America, Ruthie. I know. I go to the pictures regular. When the war's over and we go there, then – so OK – you cut nails.' He looked round the room as though seeking applause for the generosity of his decision. 'In the meantime we got to win this rotten war, no? It stands to reason. And how will cutting nails help to win the war? Is it logic? . . . Of course not. You want a nice job local. Save money on fares.' Inspiration: 'And no travel in the blackout.'

Granny Abrams: 'And you also find a nice Yiddisher Rothschild local. Marry. Settle down. Also no fares.'

'Getting married is like dying,' said Aunt Zillah drily. 'There's no hurry.'

As Mendel glared at his wife, my mother hurriedly shouted: 'Jake the Ripper!' When the rest of us gaped at her, she added: 'It's dangerous in the dark. Remember from Jake the Ripper. You don't know the palpitations I get before you come home every night. So listen to your Uncle Mendel.'

Ben spoke. 'Don't worry, Ruthie. I'll give you my bayonet. Or a truncheon. I'm making some from old broomsticks down in the cellar.'

Another scream from my mother. 'Bayonets! Truncheons! You gone potty?'

Ben, amiably, 'I thought I went. Years ago.'

'You get a job local,' my mother ordered Ruth. Suddenly pleading: 'Haven't I got enough aggravations? Enough heartache? Is it such a marvellous life I got, without worrying about you being chased by Jake the Rippers in the blackout with musical nail files or whatever? For once in your life do something to please me and get a job local.'

'Mind you,' said Granny Abrams, 'it wouldn't be such a bad thing to marry. At Ruthie's age I wasn't only married, I had children.'

'So if I did marry,' Ruth countered, 'and he gets called up for the Army, what sort of a life is that?'

'You'll get an allotment,' said Ben.

'You mean I got to spend the war growing vegetables if I get married?'

Ben scratched his head. 'I don't know from vegetables. I mean from money. From his pay.'

'And if he gets killed?' Ruth demanded.

Mendel patted her shoulder. 'Don't worry. You get the widow's pension.'

My mother's howls caused the window panes to rattle. 'How can you talk like that? You – Mendel – the businessman. The genus. Here's poor little Ruthie, your own niece, not yet eighteen, not yet engaged, not even married, and you're already making her a widow. There aren't enough of us in the family? Look at me, f'rinstance.'

Mendel looked. 'You're still a handsome woman, Minnie. You could still find some nice Yiddisher man to settle down with.'

Instead of the rage I expected, my mother held up her hands and said: 'You know why fingers are the shape they are?'

'Fingers? Shape? What's with the riddles?' asked Mendel.

'I asked if you know why fingers are the shape they are?'

Mendel shrugged. 'So all right. I don't know. Tell me.'

'So you can stuff them in your ears when madmen talk rubbish.' And with forefingers firmly jammed into her ears my mother left the room.

Nagging and hysterics won the day. Ruth found a job in the office of a Whitechapel Road manufacturer who had transferred from gowns to ATS shirts. The money was better than as a manicurist in Kilburn, there was only a minimal amount of travel in the blackout, and she transferred dreams of cutting the cuticles of a Jewish millionaire to the possibility of being wooed and won by Bernard Karp, her new employer's younger son.

Only one problem remained: me.

For my part, ambitious to become a writer at some vague time in the future, I was unconcerned about what I did in the meanwhile.

For Uncle Ben's part, he was bitterly disappointed that I did not falsify my age and join the Army, even offering me a course of bayonet practice in the back yard by way of helping me win quick promotion to the front line.

For Uncle Mendel's part, the responsibility belonged to the local Labour Exchange. 'What else are they there for if not to find Simey a job? It stands to reason. Me, I got other things to worry about. Like with a consignment of matches coming. A hundred gross boxes. From Sweden, which is abroad.' His chest swelled. 'I'm what they call the importer. I got from almost less than nothing because the ship they was travelling in nearly got sunk with bombs, and they got soaked. So you can't use from matches.'

Aunt Zillah groaned. 'Another bargain! . . . So say: what good are they?'

Mendel smirked and tapped a forefinger against his forehead. 'That's where regular going to the pictures comes in. And for why? Because I cut the ends off and sell to the posh hotels up West. In them places they'll use to stick in olives.'

My mother, incredulous: 'Stick in olives?'

Uncle Mendel: 'So sure I should live to see Hitler go bankrupt, I seen with my own eyes.'

My mother, grudgingly: 'Well, if you seen with your own eyeballs . . . And now also an important from Sweden . . . Even so . . . Well, I mean . . . Olives stuck with anchovies and them red things I also seen with my own eyeballs. But matchsticks? You mean them posh gentles eat olives stuck with matchsticks? Wood?' A sharp intake of breath. 'It could be dangerous. The splinters . . . Although, like I always said, if people don't eat Kosher it's like dust and ashes.' With a pointed look at Aunt Zillah: 'Sometimes, even when they do cook Kosher.' She shrugged. 'So anyway, if gentles eat dust and ashes, why not also sawdust?'

'Not to eat,' said Mendel irritably. 'To pick up with.'

'They haven't fingers all of a sudden?' asked Granny Abrams.

My mother, smugly: 'Like I said the other day: all that manicuring.'

As an exasperated Uncle Mendel opened his mouth, Herschel said: 'Dad, if you're interested, I know of a millionaire who's got cameras going cheap.'

Uncle Mendel's eyes narrowed with suspicion. 'Cameras? Cheap? Millionaires? What millionaires? Since when have you known millionaires? So who? Speak! Say!'

'Woolworth's. You know – nothing over sixpence. So these cameras are in three parts. Sixpence each. For one-and-six . . .' Chaos as my cousin tried to explain that he was only jokingly trying to get one-and-six from his father for a camera, while Mendel belaboured him with his fists and Zillah with her tongue – until Granny Abrams cried: 'Enough already!'

When calm had been restored, my grandmother continued: 'For my part, the best thing would be for Simey to learn a trade.'

'What trade?' my mother demanded. 'If aggravations was a trade he'd have more branches than David Greig. But otherwise?'

'A trade,' Granny Abrams persisted. 'With a trade you always earn a living. People have got to have hair cut, trousers made, beds to sleep on. Even coffins to be buried in (may it never happen here). Think of all the trades mine poor husband had (may he be sitting on God's left hand). Tailoring, wet fish, dry fish, drapery, sweets and tobacco, fish-and-chips – and more I can't remember now.' Thoughtfully: 'Mind you, it doesn't pay to be too sure of yourself.' She quoted the Yiddish proverb: 'When the shoemaker is out of work he also goes barefoot.'

'He should take a job to help the war,' said Uncle Ben.

'And if it's over any minute now?' my mother countered. 'What's the good of learning to make from say gas masks for the sake of argument, if nobody wants to gas us? It's a liberty, eh? . . .' She calculated on her fingers. 'Come to think of it, there's only twelve days to go, Mendel?'

My uncle frowned. 'Go to what?'

'Christmas.'

'So?'

'So then the war'll be over, God be thanked.' As one thought followed the other: 'By the way, you got rid of them things for the torches yet? After all, who's going to want torches if there isn't no blackout? As you yourself would say, it doesn't stand to reason.'

'I know what stands to reason,' Mendel growled, his face purpling. 'And I know that all over the country there's people crippling themselves left, right and centre in the blackout because they can't use their lousy torches.'

'Because they haven't got your things to go in them?'

Beating his fists on the table, Mendel howled: 'Because there's a shortage of stinking Number Eight batteries! . . . Oi, if I had the capital I'd show them how to run a war.' Bitterly: 'No batteries for my tissue paper.'

'It's such a terrible thing?' asked Granny Abrams.

'Of course it's terrible!' Mendel yelled. 'Because that's how I'm going to be done out of a fortune, and also how the *vershtinkener* Germans (may their children be orphans) could win this bloody war!'

My mother's eyes opened wide in wonderment. 'You mean your serviettes is what they call a secret weapon? I read in the *Star* in black and white only the other day that we already got one – I mean apart from the serviettes. Also pieces of paper. Only these they drop from airplanes telling the Germans that—'

'Airplanes?' Mendel bellowed. 'Who's talking about airplanes? The Germans can win this war without airplanes dropping paper or bombs or gas or nothing. All Hitler's got to do is sit on his bum (may it get splinters) until the country, all over, is crippled from falling over things in the blackout because they can't use their torches.'

'Perhaps you could invest in bandages and iodine,' said my mother. 'Although for my part I say a bowl of soup is better than all the medicines.' Helpfully: 'Maybe we could fill all them empty torches with *lockshen* soup. Eh? What d'you feel? After all, you're the businessman. You'd know.'

Mendel opened his mouth, but Granny Abrams said: 'Oil. Why not from oil? In the Old Country, who had torches? Candles we had, or lamps from oil.'

'Oil we got,' said my mother. 'There's a couple bottles nut oil in the larder. If you want – take. I'll get more tomorrow.'

'In America,' Mendel began, then shrugged,

flapped a hand, put his elbows on the table, cupped his head in his hands, and looked morosely towards the window. After some seconds: 'God alone knows where the next meal's coming from.'

My mother was immediately on her feet. 'You hungry? You want I should cook you some *wurst* and eggs? Or fry a nice middle plaice? It won't take a minute. When I got it this morning it was so fresh the eyes was winking at me. Or maybe a bowl barley soup? I made with ten pounds bones. A lovely taste, even if I say so myself. Strong like iron. Or—'

Mendel interrupted with a groan and a baleful glare. 'And when the food in the kitchen's used up? What then?'

My mother stared at him, uncomprehending. 'What then? Then I go to buy more.'

'With what money?' Hurriedly: 'Until I sell my matchsticks.'

'Money? . . . *Aaaah*, I follow. So it's up to you, Mendel.'

'Sure it's up to me,' he replied bitterly. 'But where do I get money?'

'Money? Who's talking about money? All you got to do is get rid of the budget and we'll eat like King George Fifth.'

'God will provide,' said Granny Abrams absently. 'Like he always has done, thank God.'

'God will provide,' my mother echoed. 'So would it kill Him to provide Mendel with a few of them Number Eight batteries, and Simon with a decent job?'

In the event the problem of my employment was rationalized: since the war was to be over in a matter of days when we'd go to America where, with Herschel, I'd help my uncle press buttons and read ticker-tapes, any temporary job would suit me. So I went to work for Sid Posner who owned a gent's outfitters in Commercial Road.

When Christmas passed and the Germans still hadn't surrendered, my mother asked Mendel what had gone wrong. Cautiously: 'You maybe made a mistake?' As Mendel's face went beetroot, she added quickly: 'I don't blame you personal. Them Germans misled you, eh?' Or that swinehound in the Town Hall. You think maybe he's in it with them? I mean, he sees a Yiddisher fellow with eyeballs come along and he tries to pull wool over them. And even if he isn't actual German, they're all the same, them dogs'-bodies: councils, town halls, mayors – they're all anti-semitic toerags.'

Mendel was quick to agree. 'You can't trust anyone these days. Spies, agents, double-crossers. Don't trust no one, Minnie. They could all be working for the Germans. All of them.'

'All? Even Yiddisher people?'

'Sometimes they pretend to be Jewish,' said Mendel darkly.

My mother scratched her head. 'Pretend? To be Jewish? What's the bargain wanting to be persecuted the rest of your life?'

'Like I said: they pretend.' He nodded his head. 'You'd be amazed the things these Germans get up to. Amazed. I know. I seen this picture from the Ministry that's on down the road with the picture about the lost planet – only the one from the Ministry was about a man who can't sleep because he don't trust banks and keeps bundles of money under the mattress (I should have such bad nights!). So anyway, thousands he had. Thousands! May God give me stones in the kidneys if I lie, but he got thousands in canvas bags under the mattress so it looks like them mountains on the lost planet in the other picture I also saw. Mountains up to the sky. So sure I should have a good year – up to the sky.

'So he thinks to put it in the Post Office Savings, like the Government says, because apart from not sleeping and so can't do his job proper as a part-time fireman, what if him and the money get bombed to pieces? Eh? What can you do with money that's been blown to

Timbuctoo? So the Post Office. But this other man – the one with a monocle who's a personal friend, and is also the village grocer – says: "But what if the Post Office gets bombed?" So he don't put it in the Post Office, and the country can't borrow it to buy bombs to drop on the *scheispot* submarines, and—'

'Wait a minute,' my mother interrupted, raising a hand. 'What's this to do with the man at the Town Hall?'

'I'm trying to tell you,' Mendel wailed. '*Oi veh* . . . In America Nelson Eddy's got thousands of niggers on their bended knees so silent you can hear a pin drop every time he opens his mouth to sing. So sure my children should marry: a pin. And do I want to sing? Do I? All I'm asking is to finish one lousy sentence – and I'm not even asking you to go on your bended knees, am I?'

'A good job too,' my mother retorted. 'With mine arthritis I'd never get up again . . . So go on. Drop pins. I'm listening.'

Mendel sighed. 'So why doesn't this man with the monocle who's a village grocer want the other man to put the money in the Post Office? Because he's a lousy Nazi, that's why.'

My mother whistled with astonishment. 'Never! . . . But how do you know?'

'Because at the end of the picture he goes for a wash and you see, in black and white, that he's got a swastika tattooed under his arm.'

Another whistle, a thoughtful pause, then: 'I'm not surprised.'

Mendel stared at her. 'I was surprised and you're not? How come?'

'I don't know from villages, but villages, towns, countries – are grocers so different from butchers? What else you expect? . . . Anyway, you got the answer, no? Quick as a flash. Eyeball to eyeball in black and white.'

'Huh?'

'On Friday you follow this filth from the Town Hall to the baths and take a look under the armpits. Only be careful. It could be dangerous. Mind the eyeballs . . . Course, he might be one of them people who doesn't go to the baths Friday regular, or does tops and bottoms in a basin at home. So report him to the Town Hall. Let them have the aggravations for a change.' She frowned, then shrugged. 'So maybe not the Town Hall, but the Air Raid Warden at number thirty, or the Secret Service. Or I'll get Mrs Krenk write a postcard. Or ask from Ben. He was in the Army, now the ARP. So he'll know what to do.'

'Ben!' Mendel snarled. 'He knows nothing.'

'So he's the lucky one,' said my mother.

Mendel's eyebrows seemed to rise to the top

of his forehead. 'Lucky? He knows nothing, yet he's lucky? How come lucky?'

My mother smiled and patted his shoulder. 'I'm remembering what our poor father, may he rest in peace, used to say from the Yiddish: he's lucky because he doesn't know that he doesn't know.'

One afternoon in January my mother accepted an invitation to have tea with Mrs Klopps. Such an occasion always brought misgivings. 'For one thing, it means Zillah has got to help out with the supper. Thank God the meat's done – the cold chicken. But the veg is roast potatoes. And you know what that means, eh? Heartburn for a fortnight. You'd think that by now she'd be able to roast a rotten potato. But no. So for afters we got bicarb.'

For another thing, my mother was appalled that when she went to tea with Mrs Klopps (or Mrs Block or Ada Krenk or Rosie Speck) the invitation meant more or less just that: not a table concave under the weight of food, but cups of tea accompanied by bread and butter and jam, and maybe biscuits or a slice of cake. 'For my part I couldn't care less,' she assured me as she adjusted her hairpins. 'Like you know, I eat less than a sparrow.'

'Then why complain?' I asked.

She beat me about the head with her hand

mirror – until, with a howl: 'So that's it, eh? You're trying to bring me seven years bad luck!' As she put down the mirror, a hollow laugh. 'So what's another seven years?' She shrugged and turned to me. 'But to say I complain. *Me . . . Complain?* When have I ever complained? . . . Complain yet! . . . Oi, to have given birth to such filth! Such a mother-hating Cossack! . . . Complain . . . You should be ashamed of yourself.' Having asked the ceiling why He had cursed her with such a son, and why she had to suffer the aggravations of widowhood, and having demanded to know why there was no one to advise and guide, and having received no answer, she said: 'It's the principle.'

'What is?'

'Tea is. After all, tea is tea. So all right, if you're thirsty, a cup of tea. But otherwise? It's not nice.' To demonstrate what she meant my mother plundered the larder of *strudel*, cheesecake, fried fish and pickled herring, assuring herself that Granny Abrams and Uncle Mendel would have a collective fit if she went visiting empty-handed.

Since she was nervous of crossing even our cul-de-sac in the blackout, I accompanied her to Mrs Klopps's flat.

Her cronies were there, with the exception of Rosie Speck who was preparing herself for a charity ball which she was to attend on the arm of Mr Rabin, a widower who owned a cut-price glassware shop in Aylward Street.

But before this information was conveyed – indeed, hardly had the courtesies of greeting been exchanged – an excited Mrs Block asked: 'What about the news then, Mrs Ashe?'

'What news?'

'In the papers tonight. I thought you was the great one for reading all the papers cover to cover.'

'Who reads more than me? But not necessary today's papers. It depends what the lousy tradesmen wrap the food in. For you it's different. You can afford today's papers – and why not, with the money your husband must've left, being a butcher? So just say. What's so special?'

'Rationing, missus. They're starting with the rationing.'

My mother whistled. 'Never!'

Mrs Block waggled a rolled-up copy of the *Evening News*. 'See for yourself.' She unrolled the paper and read: 'Bacon and ham, four ounces a week each, and—'

'Bacon and ham?' my mother interrupted. 'That they can go on rationing 'til kingdom come. For a minute you had me worried.'

'Let her finish,' said Mrs Klopps. 'There's more yet.'

'Sure there's more,' said Mrs Block. 'F'rinstance sugar. Twelve ounces a week.'

My mother sucked air through her teeth. 'That's not so good,' she admitted. 'The family's very fond of sugar. What they call a sweet tooth. My mother, may she live to be a hundred-and-twenty-one—'

It was Mrs Klopps turn to interrupt. 'I thought the saying was a hundred-and-twenty. As my late husband told me: the same age like from Moses.'

'I don't want she should die sudden,' my mother retorted. 'So as I was saying, she's the same from all the people in *Der Heim* – the Old Country. In Poland they liked things sweet. Even toast she sprinkles with sugar. Mendel also. Five, six spoonfuls a cup of tea.' Her eyes narrowed. 'It only goes to show, eh? Just proves. They're all anti-semites. Like that man from the Town Hall . . . Mrs Krenk, you should write a postcard.'

'I already have today. But I'll be happy to write another if you tell me why the sugar is anti-semitic.'

My mother gave her a pitying look. 'Because Jewish people need more sugar than the rest of them. That's why. And what do they do? Take away the bacon and ham we don't want and in exchange give us less sugar. So if that isn't anti-semitism, what is?'

Mrs Krenk immediately reached in her handbag for a postcard and a pencil and began capital-lettering a message to the Prime Minister, silently mouthing her words between pencil-licks.

'And that's not all,' said Mrs Block. 'Butter. We got from four ounces a week each.'

Mrs Klopps sniffed. 'In the First War, there was also butter short. I remember we'd eat bread and scrape with the butter underneath so it touched the tongue first and had more taste. Remember, Mrs Ashe?'

'That I don't remember,' said my mother firmly. A contemptuous shrug. 'Whoever heard of such a thing: eating upside-down? With mine arthritis I got to stand on my head to eat a slice bread and butter? I'd rather go without.' A moment's thought, then: 'So the rich'll still eat all the butter they want.'

'I remember the First War,' said Mrs Krenk, raising her head from her postcard. 'They mislaid my poor husband.'

Ignoring this, Mrs Klopps said: 'The rich always eat. You're right there, Mrs Ashe.'

Mrs Block: 'Even with rationing? How come?'

My mother threw up her hands. 'Be reasonable. In an area like this, or where I was living in Kilburn – another poor area – how many people bought from four ounces butter each a week? Madness, huh?' When the others nodded their acceptance of the logic of this: 'So if, for the sake of argument, there's a thousand people in the East End, there's a thousand rations, no? But if only five hundred people can afford the butter there's five hundred other rations to be bought. So the poor is the poor, and they go without like they've always gone without – and the rich eat like the Duke from Westminster. As Mendel would say, it stands to reason.'

I ventured: 'But rationing doesn't work like that, Mum. If people don't take up their ration of something nobody else is supposed to have it.'

My mother nodded her head at each of her friends. 'Another genus in the family,' she said with heavy irony. 'This clever Dick' (she jerked a thumb at me) 'thinks that every lousy grocer from here to Timbuctoo is going to post back to the King from England the butter he doesn't sell . . . That'll be the day! I only wish I should live long enough to see it.'

'It'd melt,' said Mrs Block knowingly. 'And the King'll give a thank you for sending him tons of melted butter? Because there's not only the East End, there's all over. So there he is, knee-deep in melted butter.'

'Maybe Mendel could take,' said my mother thoughtfully. 'Do the King a favour.'

But rationing did not become much of a reality for my mother until March . . .

FIVE

'I just heard on the next-door wireless,' said Ben as he lumbered into the dining room and sat down.

'What did you hear?' Mendel demanded.

'Meat.'

Mendel nodded. 'So now we got a new secret weapon: talking salt beef.'

'It's going to be rationed,' said Ben placidly.

My mother gasped. 'Never!'

'So sure I'm standing here,' said Ben.

'I never heard,' Mendel growled.

'You wasn't listening to the wireless.' Ben looked slyly at his brother. 'Maybe for you they won't ration until you see with your own eyeballs personal at the pictures in a few weeks time . . . one-and-tenpence-worth a person a week.'

My mother bit her lip. 'One-and-tenpence-worth each? That's not a lot . . . They must be potty.' It did not take long for the rage to come. 'One-and-ten? What can you buy for one-and-ten? You know the price of calves' liver? Three-and-six a pound I paid yesterday (and it wasn't all that marvellous) and how far does a pound of liver go? So instead of the Germans bombing us to death, this rotten Government wants to starve us to death. Mendel, you've got to put a stop to it.'

'At least you'll be able to keep to the budget now,' said Aunt Zillah sweetly.

'Not liver,' said Uncle Ben.

My mother frowned. 'What not liver?'

'It's not rationed. It's . . . His face screwed up as he strove to remember the word. Finally: 'Offal. Heart and liver and tongue and things. Not rationed.'

My mother beamed. 'Then that's not so bad.' Her smile did not last long. 'But how am I going to manage for *lockshen* soup?'

Granny Abrams: 'We could keep chickens out the back like we did in Poland.'

'That's all we're short of,' said Aunt Zillah.

'Chickens also aren't rationed,' said Uncle Ben.

'Not rationed?' A gasp of relief from my mother. 'Even so, any rationing already . . .

One-and-tenpence . . . A stinking one-and- . . .' Her voice trailed away to head-nodding silence, then returned with a shrill '*Ah-ha!* So that's it!'

'W-what is?' asked a shaken Uncle Mendel.

'Anti-semitism.'

'Uh—'

'Otherwise why give Yiddisher people only one-and-ten?'

'But . . . but doesn't everyone get one-and-ten? Eh, Ben?'

When Ben nodded, my mother shouted: 'That's it. Like I said: anti-semitism. For they should give Yiddisher people more than one-and-ten.' After a questioning grunt from Uncle Mendel, she explained: 'Kosher butchers (the dogs'-bodies) are always more expensive than gentles, no? So for one-and-ten we'll get less meat. As you yourself would say, it stands to reason. It's logic.'

The other nodded and Aunt Zillah said: 'Always the Jews suffer. Like with the sugar.'

Granny Abrams said in Yiddish: 'Yet we survive.' A hollow laugh. 'Sometimes I wonder if it's worth it, but we survive. It's God's will we survive, so who's to argue? They treat us like dirt, but like it says in Torah, dirt lasts longer than gold.'

'So what are you going to do about it, Mendel?' my mother asked.

‘About the dirt?’

‘The one-and-tenpence.’

‘Me? Do?’ Mendel bellowed. ‘What can I do?’

My mother: ‘*Sssh*, don’t aggravate yourself. It’s just that I thought . . . well . . . I mean, with you being the businessman, I thought that maybe like that’ (she snapped her fingers) ‘in a flash. Quick as an eyeball. I mean, if you can’t advise, who can?’

Uncle Mendel accepted the wisdom of this by inflating his chest and finger-sharpening his moustache-ends. With a nod: ‘You’re right, Minnie. Who else, if not me? I’ll see what I can do.’ Delicately stroking the boils on his neck he added hopefully: ‘In the meantime maybe your Mrs Krenk could write a postcard to the Chief Rabbi?’

Aunt Zillah: ‘We should stock up.’

‘Stock up?’ her husband retorted. ‘How stock up? Where stock-up?’ He groaned. ‘In America they got what they call ice-boxes. Big like them radiograms you see at Stone’s ’lectric. Everyone’s got them. Everyone. So sure Hitler should be constipated and then get diarrhoea for life – everyone. Even taxi drivers. May God strike me dead and then blind me for life if I lie: there was this taxi driver played by Don Levy had one as big as our kitchen. As big as our kitchen – just the ice-box. And every morning Whatsit Jones – the one that sang the Donkey Serenade in the other picture, only this time he delivered the ice while he sang them Italian areas – every morning, so sure as I live and breathe, he brought fresh ice. Ice. Fresh. Every morning. For a lousy taxi driver. But me? What do I get delivered? Bills.'

My mother: 'Don't upset yourself. If these ice things are big like you say – big as the kitchen – what's the good? How do I get in to cook?'

Zillah: 'When your Aunt Hannah (may she rest in peace) came from America, wasn't you going to make an ice-box? From an orange box and ice from the fishmonger?'

'Talking about fishmongers reminds me,' said my mother quickly. 'All Ruda got today was whiting. So now we're supposed to eat whiting for fish?'

Ben: 'The trawlers are busy sweeping mines.'

My mother: 'Sweeping . . .' She shrugged. 'So while they're sweeping (sweeping yet!) they can't maybe sweep a few halibut?'

Ben, as he sniffed at the tulips that patterned the wallpaper: 'You got to register.' After various expressions of puzzlement from the rest of us, he added: 'With the butcher.'

My mother smacked the palm of her left

hand against her forehead half-a-dozen times. 'So just tell me. Just say: Who's going potty? I got to . . . What's it? Registrate? With the butcher? To get halibut? What new madness is this?'

'Meat,' said Ben equably. 'Meat. You got to decide which butcher you want to go to.'

Herschel spoke. 'I also heard on the wireless. What Uncle Ben means is that if everybody's got a ration with a particular butcher, the Government's knows how to share the meat out. One butcher gets so much, another butcher another lot, according to the number of customers. So the meat is shared round. But they got to know how much goes to a particular butcher, and the only way to know is for people to register – say which butcher they want to buy from.'

When this had been repeated, simplified and digested, the horrendous implications brought screams that must have been heard in Hackney. 'Fascists!' my mother bawled. 'Madmen! Dogsbodies! *Scheispots!*' When collective efforts had achieved some semblance of calm, she gasped breathlessly: 'Butchers . . . We all know from butchers, eh? The lousy toerags . . .' A further thirty seconds in this vein, then her shoulders slumped. After more comforting, she took a handkerchief from her apron pocket, dabbed at her eyes, blew her nose and explained: 'It's not enough to have aggravations I'd only wish on Hitler. It's not enough to be a widow. It's not enough to have arthritis. It's not enough to have butchers . . . But no! I got to pick from just the one. It's like asking me to go to the Chamber of Horrors to pick a favourite murderer.

'We all know that butchers – even Kosher butchers – are Satan's Cossacks. You got to fight them left, right and centre . . . Butchers! Why else do they call Hitler a butcher? Eh? Why never a cabinet-maker or a tailor? Eh? Tell me that. So to have one butcher? . . . You go one to the other, to this to that. From one you buy bones, from another chickens. From a third veal, and another beef.'

A weary sigh as she threw up her hands. 'If you don't know by now you'll never know. But . . . but to have no choice in the matter? To have to buy from only the one butcher? He'll have you in his pocket . . . And which butcher? . . . *Which?* Tell me that, eh? . . . So OK – Mendel, you're the genus. *You* tell me.' Folding her hands across her chest: 'Just say. Just tell. Advise and I'll do. Tell us which lousy *vershtinkener* butcher and I'll take the advice from your eyeballs . . . Just say.'

'*Oi veh,*' said Uncle Mendel.

My mother, tight-lipped: 'I don't know

from a butcher called *oi veh*. But tell me where he is and I'll go registrate.' She raised a hand. 'So long I haven't got the responsibility.'

Granny Abrams: 'Sontag?'

'Hunchback Morrie? For bones he's not bad,' my mother conceded. 'But for veal?' A *pshaw* of contempt.

Zillah: 'Levy sells nice veal.'

'Salt beef,' my mother countered. 'Levy's salt beef is stringy like pot scourers.'

'Feiner?' Mendel offered.

'Feiner?' Leaning towards him my mother said in a near-whisper: 'I got it on good authority that he can't play cards.'

Uncle Mendel's moustache-ends seemed to droop. Wearily: 'What's that to do with him as a butcher?'

'He *does* play cards,' said my mother triumphantly.

'I'm not sure I follow, if you follow me,' said Uncle Mendel hoarsely.

'Mendel, use your eyeballs. If he can't play cards, but he does play cards – for maybe thousands a night – where's the money to come from if not by robbing the customers? . . . So you decide – although such a decision I wouldn't wish on my worst enemy. But you're the head of the family' (Mendel's chest again swelled) 'so make the decision. Take the responsibility.'

‘Yes . . . Well . . .’ Sweat suddenly beaded my uncle’s forehead. ‘On the one hand . . .’ A fist crashed down on the table causing the paper flowers to jump from their vase. ‘In America—’

Granny Abrams interrupted with a raised hand and a rasp of a sigh. ‘We all know about America. But like Rabbi Pacey used to say, what’s the good counting the teeth in somebody else’s mouth?’

‘Meaning?’ Mendel growled.

‘Meaning that in America we’re not. In London we are. So there they got buttons. Here we got butchers. But like Minnie says, which one?’

‘The nearest,’ said Aunt Zillah. ‘Save the fetching and carrying.’

‘Nearest,’ Granny Abrams echoed. ‘In the old country it wasn’t a matter of nearest from furthest. In the Galicia villages we was grateful if the Kosher butcher came once a week with a horse and cart. Even in Lublin, Lodz, Cracow – even Warsaw – we didn’t pick and choose: we took the cheapest. We maybe didn’t pay, but always the cheapest. Otherwise it wasn’t fair on the butcher, no? Here in London we pick and choose not only from the butcher but the meat.’ She nodded. ‘In Poland, if the worse came to the worse, no money could mean no meat. No chickens. No nothing.

Here no money means pick and choose.' A long sigh. 'Be grateful, *kinder*: be grateful you're in England . . .'

'There's money,' said Uncle Mendel. When the rest of us looked inquiringly at him: 'I don't mean I got. What I mean to say is that people with money'll still be able to buy meat, even when the rest of us can't get. From any butcher. Like they call it on the newsreels, Black Market. Not that I'd deal with such people,' he assured us gravely, 'for the name Abrams has got respect in the East End. So would I bring shame on it?'

Granny Abrams nodded. In Yiddish she quoted: 'A good name is worth more than money.'

My mother, having considered this: 'So for money I wouldn't change my name to Hitler.' She shrugged and spread her hands. 'But for a few thousands would it be such a crime to become Smith or Jones?' She tapped her chest. 'In the heart I'd know I was still Minnie Ashe . . . A few thousands . . . Like when we was in Kilburn the vet went from Jacobson to Jack Hobson and made a fortune pretending to doctor cats.'

Impulsively I suggested: 'You'd even change your name to Butcher?' – and shrank back in my chair.

Before my mother could reply, Granny

Abrams said: 'Names. Like Minnie was saying, isn't the nearest Black that was Schwartz? The father I used to know. Manny. Always treated me fair. The son I don't know.'

'Hymie,' said Uncle Mendel. 'Hymie Black. I nearly did business with his brother in the furniture: Poxy Jack Black. The one with the holes in his face. Remember that consignment walnut veneer that got soaked when the roof blew off in the storm? Mittenberg collected on the insurance so he let me have for next to nothing. When it dried out it was all twisted up. So what good's twisted walnut veneer?' Having heard the story a dozen or more times, nobody rose to the bait. Undeterred, Uncle Mendel went on: 'You don't know? So I'll tell you. Because that's where being a business-man comes in. Where you can learn lessons. You got to make snap judgements. Like that.' He snapped his fingers. 'For if you got twisted veneer, you go on twisting it. Roll it up like cigars. And then you no longer got just veneer, you got solid walnut table legs . . . Or even for cripples.'

This was a new addition to the story, and Aunt Zillah asked: 'Cripples? Walnut veneer for cripples? You invented some crazy new bandages?'

A self-deprecatory shrug. 'I got to admit it

wasn't me personal, but Leslie Banks. 'Cause in this picture when he was from the government in Africa, and when all them darkies got their legs bit off by that mad crocodile (may it never happen here), they needed wooden legs. So he used chair legs from the local school. You follow?' When the response to his question reflected varying forms and degrees of bafflement, Uncle Mendel explained: 'So if not armchair legs, this veneer could be rolled into special solid walnut legs for rich cripples. In Mayfair and Finchley there must be cripples crying out for such legs.' He shrugged. 'Only by the time I'd seen this film, Poxy Jack didn't want the veneer and I'd sold elsewhere.'

After much head-shaking, indicating that Poxy Jack Black symbolized a world lunatic in its unawareness of the genius of Mendel Abrams, my mother said: 'I wish I had your brains.'

Uncle Mendel beamed at her and tapped his forehead. 'Either you got it up here or you haven't.'

'You got it all right,' my mother breathed. 'So say – which butcher do I go to?'

Uncle Mendel's face fell. 'Yes . . . Well . . . Um . . .' He chewed at a thumbnail. 'Why not give Hymie Black a try?'

My mother raised her hands. 'OK. Fine. Sure. If that's what you want.' She looked at the rest of us in turn. 'You're witnesses. You heard in black and white: Hymie Black. So don't blame me.'

'Blame?' Granny Abrams echoed. 'For what blame?'

'With butchers there's always blame,' my mother retorted. 'Only this isn't my responsibility. Mendel says to registrate with Black, so we'll registrate . . . So that's that. Now who wants a cup of tea? With maybe a nice quarter cold chicken . . .?'

Mendel did register us with Hymie Black, and on the day after that momentous event I was summoned from my bed at the first glimmer of dawn.

'What's the matter?' I asked.

'You can come with me on the way to work,' my mother replied.

'Come? Where?'

'Where? The butcher. Where else?'

'Why?'

'Why?' She sighed. 'If you don't know I'll tell you. I'm a widow, right? Not only crippled from arthritis, but with no proper man to stand up for me. Mendel's got business to attend to. Ben's helping – as well as being up half the night with the ARP – so who's to be my witness? Take my part?' Although I felt that single-handed she could hold her own (and more) in most of her battles with butchers, I said nothing. She went on to explain: 'It's this rationing. Registrating. Before, if a butcher done me dirt I'd go elsewhere. But now I need witnesses.'

'How will witnesses help?' I asked.

She sighed at my ignorance. 'Because, clever Dick, it said on the wireless last night that if a tradesman doesn't give full rations he can be locked away by the police. So even if he robs me blind, what can I do unless I got a witness?' An empty laugh. 'His word against mine? They're such liars, these butchers, they'd even put up a good argument with the Angel of Death.' Briskly: 'So try to act like a *mensch* – a man. Like your poor father would've done (although I should be punished for daring to mention you and him in the same breath). But who else is there? So have a wash, eat your breakfast and come.'

I washed, ate, and went.

As we walked along Zanzibar Terrace, my mother said: 'I'll tell you another thing from the wireless: for wasting food there's a hundred pound fine and three months in prison every time you do it. So a good job your Aunt Zillah isn't doing the cooking, eh? Mendel would be bankrupt for every penny, and she'd spend the rest of her life doing hard labour.' She nodded thoughtfully as she considered the latter punishment.

Hymie Black's shop, in an alley off Cable Street, was much the same as those of other small butchers in the area: shadowed by shutters, fly-buzzing, redolent of a composite of damp, drains, meat, poultry and sawdust. The butcher was a heavy, mournful, stooping man in his forties, an extraordinarily narrow crescent of a nose hooked over the moustache of his grey-bearded face, a greasy skull cap perched on thinning, grizzled hair, and who had the nervous habit of tunelessly whistling through his teeth and drumming his fingers on the chopping block while listening to people. His wife, Dora, was stout and squat and equally morose-looking, her head nodding in rhythm with her husband's finger-tapping.

To my surprise, my mother did not sweep into the shop arrogantly Queen of Sheba; nor with umbrella aloft and eyes blazing, like a wild-haired, aproned and slippered Goddess of Vengeance. She sidled in, almost shy and apologetic: her Hard-Done-By-Widow role. She explained that she had no man to stand up for her . . . That although she'd had some nasty experiences with butchers, she was prepared to forgive and forget and give Black a fair chance . . . That if he treated her right she'd arrange for him to have cheap some yellow paint for the gassing, doilies for the torches, even sand for the floor in case the sawdust ran out . . . That in times like these Yiddisher people had got to stick together . . . That it was possibly not his fault he was a butcher: after all, some people had to do the dirty work like clean the lavatories and commit the murders . . .

I felt that this attempt at ingratiation could not last long. Nor did it. After two minutes, a lightning change of mood, and she informed Hymie Black that her brother was an important business genus who went to the pictures regular so knew what was going on in the world . . . That another brother was a Great War hero with medals and very high-up in ARP . . . That if he didn't watch his step she'd arrange for a postcard to be sent to the King . . . That she knew a woman who was married to a butcher who, because of the way he carried on, died a death she wouldn't even wish on Hitler . . . 'So I'm prepared to let bygones be bygones if you treat me proper,' she concluded. 'No fingers on the scales. No short change. No stale meat if I can't come personal and have to send from one of the children. Otherwise I go straight to the police.' Jerking her head towards me: 'I got a witness. In black and white.'

Black stopped his whistling and finger-drumming to ask: 'Witness for what, lady?'

'For the short measure. Just give me that much short,' she indicated with finger and thumb, 'and I'll have you locked away for life. And they won't let you take no gold with you to stuff in the mattress.' Absently: 'Anyway, it's unlucky.'

The butcher smiled. 'In that case I'm the luckiest man in London . . . Look, lady, I don't understand from a quarter what you been creating and carrying-on about, but I can tell you this: I don't rob from nobody. I'm an honest man. I try to be a good Jew.'

'A good Jew a butcher?' my mother retorted. 'It contradicts.'

Hymie Black frowned. Sternly: 'I try to obey the law of God.'

My mother shrugged. 'It's funny eh, when you think about it.'

'What is?'

'Only one God – but a million butchers.' A shrill '*A-ha!* How do I know you're a Jew? My brother told me: people pretend. How am I to know what you got under the armpits?'

The butcher's mouth trembled. 'Ar-arm . . .' He gulped. 'Armpits? What's with armpits? And as for not being a Jew . . . *Aie, aie aie* . . . You mean Hymie Black isn't Jewish all of a sudden? When Mosley had one of his marches through the East End – remember the Battle of Cable Street? – you should have been there, lady, to tell his bastard Blackshirts I wasn't Jewish. This place they smashed to bits, and while I was trying to protect my wife and children they broke this Aryan arm.' He held out his right arm, which we now saw to be oddly twisted. 'It never set straight.'

'Yes . . . Well . . .' My mother hid her embarrassment behind an aggressive: 'So I'm sorry about your arm. But I also got arms. And legs. Also crippled. From the arthritis. But do you hear me complain all day? . . . So I haven't got time to waste . . . Chickens. They're not rationed, huh?' When the butcher's slow nods accepted this: 'I'll have two boilers.'

More nods. 'Not rationed, lady, but short.'

A dismissive '*Pshaw*. Tall, short don't worry me – so long they got from meat on the outside and fat for cooking on the inside.' As the butcher gave her a bleak look, yet reached for two boiling fowls hanging from hooks: 'I don't want plucked. I want with the feathers. Uncleaned. I know from butchers: they pluck and clean, and tear the skin and neck to shreds, and half the insides is missing – even sometimes eggs – and how can I stuff a torn neck?'

After Black had told his wife to fetch two unplucked chickens from the cellar, my mother said: 'Now I want three, four rations stewing steak.'

'Which is it, lady?' asked Hymie Black. 'Three or four?'

'Three, four. You got to count every fraction?' When the butcher said yes, 'So OK – three.' She shook her head. 'You're a hard man. A real butcher.' Her narrowed eyes did not blink or move as Black sliced and carefully weighed the meat.

'There, lady,' he said. 'Three rations stewing meat. Five-and-six. Anything else?'

It was my mother's turn to tap a finger. 'The Government, in black and white, eyeball to eyeball, says one-and-ten meat. Right? And remember I got a witness.'

'Sure it's one-and-ten. You saw I weighed.'

'One-and-ten *meat*, not one-and-ten fat!' my mother screamed – and before the butcher could intervene she grabbed his cleaver and with wild, yet astonishingly accurate blows, trimmed the fat from the meat. 'So now that's meat. The fat you can throw in extra, 'cause it isn't rationed. Just make up the rest of the ration with proper meat.'

When Hymie Black had recovered from the shock of my mother's action: 'B-but everybody's got to have fat. It *is* part of the ration.'

'Got? There's no such word as got. You can see with your own eyeballs, in black and white, there's meat lying there I cut personal with no fat. So how come got?'

Hymie Black, desperate: 'But if everyone's like you, lady, what do I do with the fat?'

'Eat it. Fat keeps you warm: I read in the paper only the other day. Save you buying coal.'

Still exercising remarkable restraint, the butcher replied: 'I can't eat it. Fat's bad for my stomach.'

My mother looked at him, incredulous. 'Bad for the stomach? So how does your stomach know if something's fat? When your wife's in the kitchen cooking, your stomach's there watching? . . . Anyway, I'm too tired to argue. I got other things to do. And my baby here' (she gave my head the relatively gentle thump that represented a kindly pat) 'has got to work to earn money to pay for this rubbish. So give me a few bones – say six, seven pounds – and I'll be off.'

I sneaked from the shop as my mother said: 'Now for mine budget,' and began the ritual of searching for pencil, paper and reading glasses before deciding how much she was prepared to pay cash and how much she'd have to owe . . .

When I arrived home that evening I learned that my mother's first action after leaving the butcher had been to go to half-a-dozen other tradesmen to check the weight of the meat Hymie Black had served her. It appeared that his scales were fractionally in her favour – and she was furious.

'Why you so angry?' asked Aunt Zillah. 'For once in your life a butcher is an honest man, and you complain. You should be grateful.'

'It's not natural,' said my mother firmly. Adding to her upset was the butcher's calm. 'I gave him what for, and he doesn't only not answer back, he adds to the ration. It's not natural I tell you.' She bit her lips and shook half-clenched fists. 'If only I could put my finger on it. Find out. He should be watched. Followed. Reported to them Secret Service people. They should keep an eye on him. He's hiding something.'

'I'll go beat him up,' said Ben, shadow-boxing the standard lamp. 'Give him what for. *Bang! Bang!*'

'*Oi gevult!*' my mother howled.

'It's already all over the East End, what you done today,' said Uncle Mendel sternly. 'This going round testing scales.' His chest swelled. 'For a man in my position it's very embarrassing.'

My mother: 'Like Nathan used to say (may he rest happy in Paradise), it's better to be embarrassed than ashamed . . . So anyway what's that butcher up to?'

For my mother, as for thousands of other women, the answer came in a matter of weeks when offal disappeared from butchers' counters. An apologetic Hymie Black: 'If the wholesaler doesn't supply, what can I do?'

My mother, with a reflex cliché of the day: 'What you got under the counter?'

'My feet,' said Hymie Black wearily.

My mother shook her head and clicked her teeth. 'A pity – I'm not allowed to eat pork . . . So what's in the 'fridge and the cellar. Out the back?'

'You want to look, lady? You're welcome.'

'And upstairs?'

'You're also welcome.'

'If I wasn't crippled from arthritis I would look.' A long sigh. 'So it's the Black Market, eh? I got it on good authority that's where it all goes.' Another catch-phrase of the time: 'But this war won't last for ever. You know that? And I won't forget in a hurry.'

'May you live to remember for another hundred years,' said the butcher equably. 'Now I'll tell you what I can give you. I got sausages. You want two pounds?'

'Sausages!' my mother sneered. 'Your sausages got so much bread I never know whether to put on mustard or butter . . . OK, I'll take two pounds . . . So these days they make animals with no tongues, no tails, no livers (I only wish they made butchers the same way), but tell me one thing – they still got bones?'

Hymie Black reached under the counter for a shin bone. My mother nodded approvingly – until he sawed-off a six-inch length with which he presented her. 'W-what's this?' she croaked.

'A bone, lady. From the shin.'

'What am I supposed to do with that?'

'What you normally use a shin bone for?'

'Make soup.'

'So make soup.'

'Soup? *Soup?!* With one lousy fragment bone? For soup you need eight, ten pounds. And not just shin. Marrow you need, and knuckle. From – from *that* I'm supposed to make soup for a dozen people? And spare for the Thermoses? You gone potty or something?' She turned to the woman behind her in the queue. 'You heard, missus, with your own eyeballs: for the whole family I'm supposed to make soup from that lousy bone. Bone did I say? A splinter to stick in the throat, more like. So say. Talk. Speak up for me. Could you make soup for a dozen people from it?'

The woman nervously fingered her necklace. 'These days I don't make soup from bones.'

My mother gaped. Respectfully: 'You . . .

you maybe the wife of one of them miracle rabbis like from the Old Country. To make soup without bones? So . . . so how does it work?'

The woman shrugged. 'I don't know from miracle rabbis – although a second cousin once removed on my husband's side was related by marriage to Ibn ben Yahudah of Lvov who had wonderful cures for the white leg. From all over they came . . . But for soup? We use veg. Carrots, swedes, onions, leeks, turnips, 'taters – whatever's going.'

'No bones?'

'I just said – no bones.'

'Then it can't be soup,' said my mother emphatically.

'What about *borsht*?' asked the woman. 'In that you got beetroot, lemon, egg. Where's the bones in that?'

'Since when was *borsht* soup?' my mother countered.

'What else is it? Cough mixture?'

'*A-ha!* That's just what it isn't, missus. Real soup, from bones or a boiling chicken, is the best medicine in the world. Including being marvellous for the coughs. Helps the throat, and I got it on good authority that that's where the coughs come from. But *borsht* for curing coughs? Whoever heard such potty ideas? Where's the strength? The iron? The goodness? A couple of bowls *borsht* with mashed p'tatoes in it is all right last thing at night for a snack, but otherwise?'

Hymie Black stopped whistling and said: 'If it's medicine you want, go register with the chemist. Me, I've only got what I'm given. So you want this bone, or don't you?'

'Sure I want. And since this wonder woman don't need bones I'll have hers.' My mother took newspapers from her basket. 'Here's paper. Now to wrap mine I want Sunday's *Referee*, the *News of the World* and Saturday's *Mirror*. The rest I got from the fishmonger, except yesterday's *Evening News* which the greengrocer promised to keep.'

When the rations were wrapped in suitable newspapers, and unsuitable arrangements were made for their payment, my mother handed me the shopping basket. 'Here, take. I haven't got the strength to carry.' To the butcher: 'I'd better say a proper good-bye. Tomorrow, with carrots serving for bones in the soup, I'm not sure I'll even have the strength to come here . . . You're going to be the death of us all, Mr Black, you realize that? Starving us to death.' She waved her umbrella at him. 'The only difference between you and the Angel of Death is that the Angel of Death doesn't charge . . .'

★

One evening, when Uncle Mendel and Aunt Zillah took Granny Abrams to visit an old acquaintance whose husband had died, and Uncle Ben was in the cellar testing home-made bayonets against coal sacks filled with sand, my mother invited her cronies for a cup of tea. She apologized for having only two choices of bread, and that the butter was so thinly spread – but she managed to produce salt, pickled and chopped herrings; biscuits, cakes, jams and anchovies; and a selection of cheeses.

I had found a gas ring in the room that was now my bedroom, so the meal was prepared there and served on newspaper-covered tea chests in the back yard, thus giving my mother some semblance of independence. 'Makes a change,' she said. 'Like from the picnics we went to at Box Hill and Higham's Park when my poor husband was alive.'

'It's certainly different,' Mrs Block agreed as, without kneeroom under the chests, she struggled to adjust herself between the dustbins and the rotting, rusting, sometimes unidentifiable detritus of Uncle Mendel's more disastrous purchases.

Bessie Klopps: 'So who was it died (may it never happen here)?'

My mother: 'Someone she knew from the Old Country. You must also have known him: Cohen the Carpenter. The one with the fingers missing. Lived off Club Row. One of the sons is in the gowns.'

Mrs Block: 'That Cohen? Never! What a shame. A nice old man. And a real craftsman. Reasonable, too. In the old days he done a lot of odd jobs for me.'

Mrs Klopps: 'And a good Jew. Never missed a Sabbath service, and always ready to make up a quorum at somebody's home for memorial prayers. He once done my sashcords.'

Rosie Speck: 'Worked his fingers to the bone. He also done for me. Hinges.'

My mother: 'Worked his fingers to the bone? Don't we all? Only with him I always thought it was the saw.'

Mrs Block appeared not to have heard this. 'I also remember Cohen the Carpenter. *Aie*, how that man worked. Did my floorboards. Day and night he worked. But lived as poor as a saint.'

'What they call pious, if you see what I mean,' said Rosie Speck. 'But I heard he was well insured. Whatever else went short, he paid the man from the Pru regular. The family'll come into money. Maybe up to five hundred pounds.'

Mrs Klopps whistled. 'Five hundred!'

Mrs Block: 'Never!'

My mother: 'I don't believe it. Five hundreds yet!' She slowly nodded her head and clicked her teeth. 'Funny, eh?'

Mrs Block: 'What is?'

My mother: 'Life is. A poor man like Cohen works day and night like a dog, and now he's dead he comes into a fortune.'

After the truth of this had been absorbed, Mrs Krenk said to Rosie Speck: 'How come you know so much about Cohen the Carpenter?'

Before Miss Speck could reply, my mother wagged a finger. 'Hold on . . . Hold hard . . . Wait a minute . . . Wasn't there some rumour about you and one of Cohen's sons?'

Miss Speck flushed and said quickly: 'There was no truth in it.'

My mother shrugged. 'It's bad enough there should have been a rumour.'

Mrs Krenk: 'What rumour?'

Mrs Klopps rolled her eyes. 'Rumour, *schmoomer*. Like my poor husband used to say—'

'Like *my* poor husband used to say,' Mrs Block interrupted, 'what *your* poor husband used to say won't pay the rent.'

Mrs Klopps: 'And what does that mean?'

Mrs Block: 'It means I still don't know what Cohen the Carpenter died.'

My mother: 'At eighty-seven how do you want he should die? Drowning while he swims the English Channel? (Although there's been stranger things.) He died in his sleep.'

'A good death,' said Mrs Block.

'There's no such thing,' my mother retorted. Suddenly slapping my face: 'Just like there's no such thing as a bad mother. You hear, you ungrateful swine?'

After my mother had been calmed, the conversation became general: progress reports on aches and pains; lamentations about rationing and shortages and the call-up of nephews and cousins; and the exchange of other titbits of topical news. Mrs Block reported the shameful case of an old man who caused consternation at air raid drill: when he put on his gas mask the magnificence of his beard caused him to near-suffocate. 'So these masks is more anti-semitism, no? For who else has long white beards except religious Jews? For such people they should have special big masks, or with holes to let the beard out.'

'I'll drop the King and the Chief Rabbi postcards,' Mrs Krenk promised, nodding her head with hairpin-loosening vigour.

'A long white beard doesn't make a man religious,' said my mother sagely. 'It only means he's old.'

'I heard of a case like that,' said Mrs Klopps. 'Only a woman.'

'With a long white beard?' squealed Rosie Speck.

'No, no, no,' said Mrs Klopps. 'A religious

woman with a gas mask. You're supposed to carry the gas mask all the time, right? But on the Sabbath you're not supposed to carry anything, are you? Not if you're all that religious.'

'For my part I think some people carry things too far,' said my mother. 'Not that I've got anything against Jews,' she added hurriedly. 'So go on with the story.'

Mrs Klopps glared. 'I'm trying . . . So if you're not supposed to carry on the Sabbath, what can this woman do?'

'She could stay home, if you see what I mean,' said Rosie Speck.

'So then she can't go to synagogue to pray.'

Almost in unison heads nodded as the awfulness of the dilemma became apparent. 'So what did she do?' asked my mother. 'Maybe go early Friday night before the Sabbath and sleep there?'

'Wouldn't work,' said Mrs Klopps smugly. 'If she did that she couldn't be home to light the Sabbath candles and make the blessings.'

'So?'

'So there was meetings with other members of the congregation and the rabbi, because at this synagogue every single one of them is as religious as her. The women shave their heads and wear wigs, and they say the men wear out three prayer shawls a week. I know: my late husband (may he rest in peace) who was assistant caretaker at the Great Synagogue, was offered a job there. He was a good Jew, but not that good. Although it was me put the foot down. It meant I'd also have to shave my head and wear a wig. And I'm told you can get terrible draughts if they don't fit proper. And with my head colds—'

'It stands to reason,' my mother interrupted. 'From where should head colds come if not the head? Can be dangerous. I read in the paper only the other day that—'

This time Mrs Block interrupted with: 'Let's hear the end of the story.'

My mother adopted her Queen of Sheba pose and Mrs Klopps went on: 'So like I was saying, they're all religious at that place.' She threw up her hands. '*Religious?* So sure I should live, they're so devout they repent *before* they sin. Just in case. Anyway, in the end the rabbi, without food or drink, stayed up all night beating himself with sticks and praying. In the morning, just in time before his heart attack, he advised that it's better to break a law of man than of God. Leave the gas masks at home, he said. If you get gassed, they'll be gassing a good Jew, and you'll go straight to Heaven in the gold chariot with no queuing. Because of your suffering. Made it sound like God was doing them a favour.'

'It's easy to die a good Jew,' said Mrs Block sententiously. 'The hard thing is to live like one.'

'Dying. Golden Chariots.' My mother groaned. 'No wonder they say gold's unlucky. But I'll tell you one thing: if they judge by aggravations then for me they got a solid-gold Rolls-Royce waiting . . . *Aie, aie, aie*, now the rabbis are doing Hitler's dirty work for him. 'Cause if everyone takes their advice – and I got it on good authority that there's Jews all over – we'll all be gassed alive in our beds and Hitler (may he grow like a potato, with his head in the ground) will be laughing up his sleeve. Another thing: it's not just gas masks you got to carry. There's yellow paint, iodine, Lysol, bandages, soup, Ex-Lax – a hundred-and-one things.' She sighed. 'So where's it all going to end? What's to become of us all? Me and my babies?' She gave my arm an affectionate squeeze that was to leave it bruised for a fortnight. 'If only there was someone to advise, to guide – and I don't mean no potty rabbi, neither. If my husband (may he be sitting at God's right hand) was here, he'd know. Quick as an eyeball. But otherwise, who is there?'

'What about your brother, the clever businessman?' asked Rosie Speck with only a hint of malice.

'Mendel?' My mother shifted uncomfortably in her chair. Embarrassment turned quickly to anger. 'Clever? Did you say *clever*? A genus, that's what he is. Really knows what's what. But them *vershtinkener* dogs'-bodies from the Town Hall are so jealous they try to bamboozle him. He'd know all right, if only they'd tell him. In the meantime, what's the answer?'

'Answer to what, if you see what I mean?' asked Rosie Speck.

'To everything. *Aie*, there used to be good fortune-tellers in the East End: tea leaves, bumps on the head, the palm, cut the cards . . . Specially the cards.'

Mrs Krenk: 'I went to a fortune-teller once. Gypsy woman. With a crystal ball. In a tent at a fair at Hackney Marshes. Cost me sixpence to find out where they'd mislaid my husband. She said for that she'd have to go into a trance which would cost me another half-crown. I told her straight that I didn't go in for that sort of superstitious rubbish.'

'I used to go regular to a woman in Fashion Street,' said Rosie Speck. 'She was always promising tall dark strangers. Well, at the dances they wasn't always tall, but being Jewish most was dark-haired, and some were certainly strange, if you see what I mean.'

Mrs Krenk: 'Maybe the good fortune-tellers

was called-up to help the government.' Darkly: 'And have now been mislaid.'

Mrs Block: 'You believe in such poppycock?'

My mother, defensively: 'Believe? Who said anything about believe? I'm just thinking . . . well, for the sake of argument, it would be nice to know for the sake of curiosity.'

Mrs Klopps: 'Like it says in Talmud: don't be so quick to worry about tomorrow. Today isn't over yet.'

Nor was it. Five minutes later Herschel arrived home with the news he'd heard on the radio at work: a massive operation was being mounted to evacuate the British Army from the beaches of Dunkirk.

SIX

That evening my mother asked: 'France isn't all that far away, is it? You should know: you passed your scholarship.'

'Maybe twenty miles or so,' I replied.

My mother whistled. 'That's not even so far from here to Westcliff. *Oi gevult*, a half-hour on the train and they'll be round the corner at Fenchurch Street.'

'What's with trains?' Mendel demanded. 'There's the sea – the English Channel to cross.'

A gloomy: 'So they'll be round the other corner – at the docks. Boats, trains – what difference? We'll still be murdered alive in our beds.'

'In the old days we'd run away to the forest,' said Granny Abrams. 'But here, where's there a forest?'

'There's Clissold Park,' said Ruth.

Herschel: 'Victoria Park.'

Ben: 'Edward Seven Memorial Park . . . And Itchy Park.'

'So how can you hide in them places from the Cossacks? You need a forest.'

'Epping's the nearest,' Aunt Zillah replied, 'but that's miles away.'

'I'll take you on the barrow,' Ben assured his mother.

'That's all I'm short of,' Granny Abrams snapped. She rocked from side to side in her chair. 'There's times I wish you was a drunkard.'

Ben shuffled his feet. 'Why d'you say that?'

'At least a drunkard gets sober from time to time. But a fool?'

'No need for drunkards, no need for barrows,' said Uncle Mendel, patting the air.

'Them Germans (may their bones go soft), they'll never get across.'

'You know something?' my mother asked eagerly. 'You heard? So tell. Explain. Don't keep us in the dark. We all want to know, and who's to tell us if not you?'

An elaborate wink, followed by a finger tapped against a nostril. 'Careless Talk Costs Lives,' he quoted. 'Walls Have Ears.' Another wink. 'You follow?'

'No,' said Aunt Zillah.

'No,' said Granny Abrams.

'No,' said my mother.

'I wish I could tell you but I can't,' said Mendel with a button-straining inflation of chest. 'I gave my word, and a Jew's word is his bondage, huh? Goes back from Egypt. Moses kept his word and they went from the Land of Bondage to the Promised Land.'

'Took forty years,' said Granny Abrams glumly. 'I haven't got that long to wait.'

'May you live to be a hundred-and-twenty-one,' my mother breathed.

'I still haven't got forty years.'

My mother patted her arm. 'OK, a hundred-and-thirty.'

'By then they'll have built a forest near Zanzibar Terrace?'

'Forests, *schmorests*!' Aunt Zillah screeched.

'Just tell, clever husband: why aren't the Germans coming?'

Mendel, wearily: 'I just said: Careless Talk. What they call Top Secret. From my source I gave my dying oath not to reveal.' Aggressively: 'You mean I'm not to be believed all of a sudden?'

Zillah dryly: 'Why "all of a sudden"?'

My uncle ignored this. 'I'll tell you this much: the other day at the pictures I saw *The Lion Has Wings* with Ralph Wassisname and the one with the moustache. So anyway, them Germans came in their airplanes, took one look at our barrage balloons and immediate turned round and went home.' He snapped his fingers. 'Quick like that. May Rothschild make me his heir and then outlive me if I lie – quick like that.'

My mother jerked a thumb towards the window. 'Them balloons I also seen. Eyeball to eyeball I see every day. But what's to do with ships?'

'Secret weapons,' said Mendel. 'When you're in business like me you make what they call contacts. And one of mine works for the Government, and—'

My mother interrupted with a shrill whistle. 'You know someone in the Government?' She gasped. '*Aie, aie, aie,* that's something. He'll maybe give you a big job, eh? Something important. Didn't I always say they could do with a Yiddisher genus like you in the Government? Like that other one, Eden, who was formerly Yidden. You'd soon put a stop to this rotten war, no? All you need is a hat like his.'

'You're right, Minnie, I could show them what for,' said Uncle Mendel emphatically. 'But this fellow isn't actual in the Government. He works for it. Sub-contracts making buttonholes for army overcoats. But he meets people. Gets to know things. Like about secret weapons.'

'So tell us,' said my mother impatiently.

'I can't. I'm sworn to secrecy. It's like with that picture from the Ministry that was showing with *The Lion*. There was this man who discovered the leakage in the lavatory.'

'That we also got,' said Aunt Zillah. 'So why pay good money to see one at the pictures?'

Uncle Mendel clenched his fists. With some effort: 'Leaking is Secret Service talk for passing. This dirty rotter was passing secrets in the lav. For money. 'Cause he was a gambler and was short of money.'

My mother: 'Talking about gambling reminds me of a story I heard the other day from the fishmonger (may his thumb press as heavy on his heart at night as it does on the scales during the day). It appears that one of his brothers was due at synagogue the other Friday for memorial prayers (may it never happen here), but he didn't turn up. Sent a message he was sick. Then they found he'd really been out gambling with the cards. So the fishmonger said to him: "You said you was sick, but all the time you was gambling." And you know what the brother replied? You know? He said: "With me it's a sickness," Funny, eh?'

We all laughed – except for Mendel who beat his head with his fists, and Granny Abrams who said: 'Can you tell again in Yiddish, Minnie?'

'Sure,' said my mother. 'But first I want to know why them Germans aren't going to come over. After all, Mendel, it's not as though any of us was going to go rushing down to the lav looking for gamblers. Does it stand to reason? Is it logic?'

'But I swore to my contact,' Mendel howled.

'And we're not contacts?' my mother howled back. 'Your own flesh and blood is not so important as from some no-good buttonhole maker? How can you be like that? How can you say such a thing?'

Mendel's shoulders slumped. 'All right. All right. But first I want everyone to swear.'

And having solemnly made us chorus: 'I swear by my life never to breathe a word, and may God strike me dead and then cripple me if I do' he whispered: 'Death ray,' and looked at us narrow-eyed. 'What d'you think of that?'

Aunt Zillah: 'What can I think if I don't know what it means?'

'It's like in the picture at the Troxy I saw,' said Mendel conspiratorially. 'The one with Boris Karloff and that other fellow who's in the wheelchair. Boris invented this machine that was so small like a cigar box – so sure I should live, not an inch bigger – yet when he pressed a button an invisible ray went out for hundreds of miles, and everybody dropped down dead.'

'Never!' my mother gasped.

'So sure I should have a good year – everybody dropped down dead . . . Until he accidental turned it the wrong way round.' Triumphantly: 'So now we got the same.' He rubbed his hands. 'If them poxy Germans try any monkey business they'll get a lesson they'll remember the rest of their lives . . . So now you see why it's Top Secret, no?'

Aunt Zillah: 'You believe such nonsense?'

Uncle Ben: 'In the last war they said tanks was nonsense. Also airplanes. But they wasn't.'

My mother, who had been thoughtfully

scratching her chin: ‘Maybe they also got a Troxy in Germany.’

Uncle Mendel frowned at her. ‘Meaning?’

‘That maybe the Germans also saw the picture and also got a cigar box.’

‘Yes . . . Well . . .’ Mendel recovered quickly with a wink and a knowing ‘Top Secret’. He twirled his moustache-ends. ‘So not a word, huh?’ Plainly anxious to change the subject: ‘And I got more news . . . Telephone d’rectories.’ Having assured himself of an attentive audience: ‘There’s a shortage of toilet paper, no?’

Aunt Zillah: ‘A pity you cut up them serviettes, or doilies, or whatever.’

Mendel glowered. ‘For them I also had ideas. With what they call a paper punch what makes holes I was going to turn them circles into confetti. But what does the *meschuggener* Government do?’ He bit at his knuckles. ‘They ban confetti. To save paper. Save? How come save? If I got confetti ready, but can’t use, where’s save? It’s waste, no? . . . So anyway, telephone d’rectories. I’ll get the kids to cut into squares, then I’ll make holes in the corner with the punch, thread bundles with string – and in no time I’ll make a fortune. Once this rotten war is over we’ll have the money to go to America and buy all the doilies you want. Because war or no war, people got to go to the lav – so why not with Mendel Abrams's telephone d'rectories?'

Ben, who had been using a fish knife and the lamp standard for bayonet practice, turned and tapped the knife against the side of his face. 'You mean them telephone books we got in part exchange for the seaside shells?'

Mendel nodded and stuck his thumbs in the top pockets of his waistcoat. 'Didn't I say they'd come in handy one day?'

'But they was going mouldy with damp.'

'We'll dry and iron them,' said Mendel airily.

'The other day you said to throw out.'

'So today I've changed my mind. That's where being a businessman comes in. Snap decisions.' He took his thumbs from his pockets and demonstrated. 'Like that.'

'You should have snapped yesterday,' said Ben flatly. 'I threw out this morning when they come collecting for salvage.'

Mendel's face went a terrifying purple, his eyes bulged, he threw his arms above his head, clawing at the air, then uttered a shrill shriek that caused the rest of us to wince.

'Mendel!' his wife screamed, 'you frightened the life out of me.'

'Nearly gave me heart failure,' said Granny Abrams shakily.

My mother nodded. 'Me, too.' With a gasp: 'You all right, Mother? You want I should make a cup of tea? Or warm up a bowl soup? It's marvellous for the heart failure. Better than all the medicines. I made fresh this morning with . . .' She checked herself and gave an apologetic shrug. 'Well, *some* bones. Not as strong as I'd like, but not too bad, even if I say so myself. And what about you, Mendel? A drop of barley soup's wonderful for the aggravations. I read in the *Jewish Chronicle* only last week.'

Mendel, his colour near normal again, but still visibly trembling, snarled. He breathed deeply for some seconds, then managed a falsetto: 'Soup? Tea?' He swallowed. In a fairly normal voice: 'I'd choke on it. Choke. You follow? Choke. May God paralyse me for life if I don't.' He nodded his head. 'Maybe that'd be for the best, eh?' Indicating Ben with a thumb. 'Let this cabbage take over . . . *Aie*, to . . . to . . . to go give away them telephone books.'

Granny Abrams, reasonably: 'I don't like to take his side, but he only done what you told.'

Mendel ground his teeth. 'All his bloody life he doesn't do what he's told, this . . . this *vershtinkener scheispot*, and when he does, what happens? He costs me a fortune.' He raised a hand. 'So all right. OK. Fine. But so sure I live and breathe, if we don't go to America, that's the one to blame.'

My grandmother threw up her hands. 'America. All the time America. Sometimes I wish God hadn't created it.' In Yiddish: 'Then again, who's to question? As Ibn Zabara says in The Book of Joy: if God in His wisdom created fleas, what right have we got to argue?'

'Then how come Rabbi Grimsvitch's home smells all the time from carbolic?' Mendel retorted.

My grandmother shrugged. 'Go ask Rabbi Grimsvitch . . . Anyway, from these telephone things you'd've made such a fortune?'

'Not just from them,' said Mendel irritably. 'But like I've said a million times, a business-man like me needs funds. Capital. And one thing leads to another. You talk of carbolic. So how did them Levy brothers start? From just one bar Lifebuoy soap they started. Now they're worth millions. From just one lousy, stinking bar carbolic soap.'

'Would I know them?' asked Granny Abrams. 'Over the years I known plenty Levys. Why not write and ask if them or their parents remember me? F'rinstance if it was the Levy your poor father gave a job when we was in the wet fish, they should be grateful. That Levy – I think it was Bernie – didn't have a farthing to bless himself 'til Aaron gave him a job. So if you remind he might give you some of that carbolic and you can start your own soap.'

'You want carbolic?' my mother asked. 'Why didn't you say? You know you've only got to ask. There's a full bottle in the cupboard. Must be more than enough for a bar soap.' Excitedly: 'You could make two, three bars, and if these Levys started with only the one, you'd catch up in no time. It stands to reason, no? . . . Simey, go quick and fetch the bottle of carbolic.'

'To tell the truth,' said Mendel, wiping a hand across his forehead, 'the way I feel now I'd probably drink it.'

'Why didn't you tell me you was thirsty?' my mother asked reprovingly. 'I'll go put the kettle on.'

Despite the death ray, the family became aware that the war was now something more than a bewilderment of inconveniences as the Government encouraged or imposed more economies and restrictions, and urged people to join the Services or Civil Defence, or transfer to jobs of positive value to the War Effort.

The first to respond were Ruth and Sybil who became part-time Red Cross workers – their choice inspired, I later discoverd, by a story in

The Oracle in which one such worker gave a wounded Guards captain a bar of milk chocolate, and he responded by looking deep into her violet eyes and would have been swept off his feet had he not been flat on his back.

Exercising enormous strength of will, the girls thereafter took their sweet rations in the form of chocolate bars, and always kept a portion ready in their handbags in the event of finding a wounded Guards captain prone on the pavement of Whitechapel High Street.

For once my mother and Aunt Zillah were in some sort of accord. After recovering from the initial shock of their daughters wanting to join anything at all, and relieved that it wasn't one of the women's branches of the Armed Services, they were proud to see them in their uniforms (although they would have been happier if the insignia could have been changed to the Star of David). They were worried at the thought of Ruth and Sybil being out for three evenings a week in the blackout with Jake the Rippers on the prowl (although they agreed that if the girls went and returned together there was some measure of security – and hastily assured Ben with shrill emphasis that the danger didn't warrant Ruth and Sybil equipping themselves with truncheons, bayonets, or stockings filled with sand and rusty nails).

And they were excited at the possibility of the Red Cross proving a means of their daughters meeting eligible Jewish doctors – and even if they didn't, wasn't the Red Cross almost the same as having a doctor in the family? So my mother now bombarded Ruth with questions, her own and those of her cronies ('I'll ask from my daughter in the Red Cross'), about arthritis, bowel movements, ingrowing toenails, lumps, varicose veins, obesity, heartburn, falling hair, pimples, bunions, and similar basic medical problems – despite protestations by my sister that her work was purely clerical.

'Clerical, *shmerical*!' my mother had occasion to retort. 'The Red Cross is the Red Cross. If not, what else is it? Eh? Bandaging, iodine. Rubbing liniment (and tonight you can do my back).' Her voice rose. 'So what have you got against helping your own mother? Just say? Huh? You mean it's not enough I'm being killed with aggravations, you also want I should die of a disease? Is that it, you ungrateful beast?' Addressing herself to the ceiling: 'So what sort of daughter have You cursed me with? A Cossack for a son isn't enough already? I'm also to be cursed with a daughter who won't cure my palpitations? But why? Just say. Tell. Explain . . .'

When no answer came she flapped a hand

in dismissal and turned again to Ruth with a savage: 'Red Cross! May specialists come from all over to learn about the sickness they name after you! For once in a blue moon, once in a lifetime, I ask advice on palpitations, and all you come out with is clerical.'

Inspired by desperation, Ruth cried: '*Lockshen* soup!'

My mother stared at her. 'What did you say? Repeat.'

Ruth, nervously: '*Lockshen* soup.' She swallowed and went on: 'Down at the station there's a doctor who says *lockshen* soup's marvellous for the palpitations.' She rolled her eyes. 'And not just for that. Honestly, down at the station they hardly talk of anything except *lockshen* soup. In . . . in fact they're working on a system to store it instead of that . . . that blood plasma I read about.'

'*Lockshen* soup certainly builds blood,' said my mother absently. For perhaps half-a-minute she sat in thought, lips pursed, head nodding, eyes staring. Then: '*Ah-ha!* So wasn't I right? Didn't I always say? May God punish me if I lie, but haven't I said all along that *lockshen* soup is the best medicine in the world (except from maybe things like the kidneys or the bile, for which barley soup takes some beating?) . . . *Lockshen* soup.' She beamed. 'So I was right. OK, so I can hardly read or write proper, don't know from my ABC, but *lockshen* soup, that I do know. Nobody can say different. And now the doctors, the specialists – even the Red Crosses – agree with me. Me, Minnie Ashe! Wait 'til the others hear!'

She rubbed her hands. 'So maybe I'll also join this Red Cross. 'Cause there's ways and ways of making *lockshen* soup. Some people,' she jerked a thumb towards the upper part of the house, 'can kill better than cure. It's got to be done proper. So I'll come show. Teach.' An elaborate, self-deprecative shrug. 'I'm no genus like your Uncle Mendel, but *lockshen* soup is another kettle of fish. So I'll come show.'

To Ruth's relief, my mother never found time to follow up this promise, but when subsequent demands for medical advice were answered by my sister with '*lockshen* soup' or 'barley soup', my mother happily and confidently passed on this information 'which I've known for myself all my life, but now I also got on good authority from my daughter in the Red Cross who's very close to the top doctors there.'

While Mendel assured everyone that he would be more than happy to help out the Civil Defence when a suitably senior vacancy occurred on the administrative side of that organization, Herschel created a major drama by leaving his job at the bakery and joining the Auxiliary Fire Service as a three-pound-a-week fireman.

Uncle Mendel's near apoplexy was inspired by the fact that for the first time in his life Herschel had taken a decision without his father's approval. 'What are fathers for,' an outraged Mendel roared, 'if not to give advice? And here I am, the head of the family, the businessman, the bread-giver, defied left, right and bloody centre. Would Micky Rooney behave in such a fashion? Would Shirley Temple? Even them Dead End Kids got more respect . . . To go behind my back. To run away to the fire station . . . Fire stations yet! A Yiddisher boy a fireman . . .'

'There's lots of Jewish firemen these days,' Herschel assured him. 'Like you know, there's plenty of Jewish taxi drivers. And thousands of taxis have been requisitioned to haul fire appliances: them grey trailer pumps. You must have seen them. So cabbies are the best people to drive them, because if there's a fire who knows where to go better than a taxi driver?'

'*Oi veh!*' Uncle Mendel cried, smacking his forehead with the heel of his hand. 'So now you're not only in the bakery and the fire, you're also a secret taxi driver.' His shoulders slumped. 'Not to ask me first, eyeball to eyeball . . .'

'I knew what you'd say.'

Mendel groaned. 'Now it's not only the bakery and the fire and the taxi driving – he's also a mind reader.' He shook his head. 'When you was circumcised I sometimes wonder if the rabbi blessed the wrong part.'

My mother, appeasingly: 'You must admit, Mendel, that he looks very smart in the uniform. And it'll also be a saving in suits.'

Mendel looked pityingly at my mother. 'So being a convict would also be a saving.' He turned, examined his son from head to toe, and uttered a contemptuous '*Pshaw!* Call that a uniform? Now in America they really got uniforms. Like Chester Morris in that picture in the forest where the trees was growing. He was a Fire Ranger, and the way he lived! Motor car. Telephone. Blackies to scrub and polish, fetch and carry – and they also what they call tap dance on the floor in white ties and tails. So the money Chester must earn! A fortune, and—'

'I'm sorry to interrupt,' said my mother, 'and I know you're a genus who must have seen with your own eyeballs in black and white – but you really mean they got people in America paid fortunes to arrange fires?

Sounds potty to me. But I suppose learning the trade how to put them out (maybe Herschel could put in a bit of practice in Epping Forest) will come in handy when we go to America. I mean to say, it stands to reason that if a fire arranger gets paid a fortune, they must pay a double fortune to the people who put them out.'

'Not arranger!' Mendel bellowed. 'I said . . .' He took a deep breath and gave an *aie-aie-aie* of a sigh. 'Forget it. It don't matter . . . Herschel a fireman.' As the rage returned: 'I should give him such a good hiding he'll remember all his born days. Beat him black and blue. Break his legs. To defy me. *Me!* Not only his father, but also Mendel Abrams. In America I'd only have to raise a little finger' (he demonstrated) 'and he'd have his head blown off.'

'Not the head,' my mother cried. 'It could be dangerous.'

When I joined the ARP as a part-time messenger, my mother's immediate reaction was of disappointment: I was not supplied with uniform or boots, only an armband. 'Trust you,' she shouted, beating me over the head with a tray of cheesecake she'd just taken from the oven. 'Trust you to make me go on buying clothes and shoes . . . So what is it, this being a messenger? Run errands?' Hopefully: 'You get tips? A few coppers here and there?' When I explained there were no tips, only the need to run messages if and when the telephones broke down, she frowned. 'That's going to kill Hitler? Or you maybe mean he's going to phone down the road to say he gives up and you go running with a message to tell the King from England?' A massive shrug. 'I don't believe it.'

'Neither do I,' I replied. 'What it means is that if the telephone exchange gets bombed, or the lines are blown down, someone's got to tell people that . . . well . . . suppose a bomb drops on Zanzibar Terrace?'

'You mean I won't know?' my mother screamed. 'I'll need you to come running with a message to tell me I'm dead? . . . Running yet. Running's very bad for the heart, you know that? I read in the *Empire News* only the other day. And one thing's for sure: if they don't supply boots, don't run too far. Repairs cost a fortune . . . Also you'll have less distance to run back . . . Running: and in the blackout, too. You must eat more fish – when I can get from the lousy fishmonger. Fish is marvellous for the eyesight. I read in the papers that them miners live on nothing else . . . Running in the blackout. God alone knows what you'll get up to. What germs you can pick up.' Her hand flew to her mouth. 'Woe is me!'

'What's the matter?' I asked.

'Women,' she breathed. Unexpectedly, she put her arms around my shoulders. 'Don't ask, just take my word: in the blackout there's women.'

'Sure there are. Men, too.'

A growl of impatience. 'I don't mean women, but . . . *women*. You follow?'

I did, but aware that an admission would inspire hysterical demands to know how and why I knew, I said: 'No.'

Another 'Woe is me'. Then her eyes widened as the answer came: 'I'll ask from Mendel to take you to one side. He'll know. He'll tell you. Explain . . . If only your poor father was alive . . . But with no man of my own, no father for my babies, we'll ask from Mendel. It's no joke, believe me, when there are questions, questions, questions – but no answers.' Hastily: 'But ask; always ask. Otherwise how else will you learn?'

My mother arrived home from a visit to Mrs Klopps, went to prepare supper – and terrified the household with a truly horrendous scream. When the rest of us arrived in the kitchen, a breathless: 'Help! Murder! Call the police. There's been robbers. Thieves! Cossacks!' She collapsed into a chair. After Aunt Zillah had fanned her with a newspaper for some seconds, my mother pointed a trembling finger towards the larder. 'G-gone. The food. It – it – it's gone. We've been robbed left, right and centre. Cleaned out.' Her voice rose to a tremulous shriek. 'Simey, don't stand like a stuffed dummy – go run a message. Ben – fetch bayonets. Mendel – go see the man in the Town Hall. Ruthie – put on the soup and the iodine . . . We've been robbed blind. The rations—'

Uncle Ben interrupted with: 'Government orders.' As we all turned and stared at him: 'You read the papers, Minnie. You always say nobody reads thorough like you. So you must know.'

My mother swallowed. 'You . . . you saying the Government's so short of food they stole my rations. Is that it?'

Ben shook his head. 'Invasion. The Government says that in case them lousy Germans land (may their bums drop off), you got to hide your food. So I hid. In the cellar. Under that load of blankets Mendel got from the Chinese Mission. So don't worry; I'll go fetch.'

This time there was a collective scream, and when it died down my mother was the first to speak. Shakily: 'In . . . in the cellar? The cellar? With the damp and the rats and God alone knows what else? . . .' She swallowed. 'God keep us alive! I knew you was soft in the head, a bit funny, but . . . but to . . . and in the cellar . . . And under them Chinese yet! Who knows what diseases they got? It'll have to be boiled, fumigated with sulphur candles. God alone knows what time we'll eat tonight.'

'I seen at the Gaumont with Charlie Chan,' said Mendel. 'Opium. Poison darts.'

'That's all we're short of,' my mother groaned. 'Poison in the mince.'

'I wrapped in greaseproof,' said Ben. 'Mind you, I didn't allow for no darts.'

Uncle Mendel clenched and unclenched his fists. 'Ben . . .' A few swallows before he was able to manage: 'Them Germans . . . So OK, cabbage, you got my permission: when they come knocking at the door you share out them bayonets and we'll all kill them. Eyeball to eyeball in black and white. May God strike me dead and then punish me with dropsy if I lie, but we'll all take one of them bayonets and cut their hearts out.' With a great effort of self-control: 'So in the meantime be a good boy, eh? Leave the food where it is? Uh? . . . OK?'

Ben shrugged. 'Please yourself, but don't be surprised if I report you to the police' – then fled from the kitchen as Mendel threw the bread-board at him.

*

With the threat of invasion, Ben certainly came into his own. After Anthony Eden's radio appeal, he applied to join the Local Defence Volunteers – people not in the Services who would man road blocks, patrol vulnerable areas, and so on. Ben was turned down: not for any medical reason this time, but because according to the rules he was a potential security risk – his father had been Polish.

When told this, he half-strangled the sergeant at Leman Street police station with one hand; with the other he pointed to his Military Medal and roared: 'I wasn't too bloody foreign to win this, was I?' – and excitedly burst into a stream of Yiddish obscenities, whereupon the sergeant, having freed and massaged his throat, said: 'See – you can't even talk English proper.'

'I was born down the bloody road, you *shmock*!' Ben screamed – and began to smash up the police station.

The incident was revealed when the amiable Police Constable Lucas, who knew Ben of old, brought him home with the assurance that no charges would be brought if Uncle Mendel promised that there would be no similar incident.

Mendel promised, but the tongue-lashing he gave Ben was relatively mild: he was inclined to agree with his brother that the police sergeant was an anti-semitic dog'sbody for whom hanging, followed by fourteen years hard labour, would have been too lenient a punishment.

Insisting that he was entitled to defend his own home, Uncle Ben found room on his uniform for another armband, this one inked VOLUNTEER DEFENDER, and took to marching up and down Zanzibar Terrace shouldering a curtain rod to which he'd tied one of his bayonets. There was general embarrassment, but my mother urged Mendel to 'leave him be, he means well' – until he was found negotiating his wardrobe down the stairs to stand outside the front door as a sentry box. 'Maybe you should have a word with him, after all, Mendel,' my mother suggested. Mendel had several words, as did Granny Abrams and Aunt Zillah.

Uncle Ben then got hold of a primitive air rifle and a supply of lead pellets. Again he attached a bayonet, and again he patrolled the street, but now took pot-shots at any window that revealed the slightest glow of blackout-infringing light. 'Could be signalling the enemy,' he explained. When Mendel scanned the sky and demanded: 'What bloody enemy?' Ben winked and replied: 'Top Secret. Walls Have Ears. You said yourself.' Fortunately,

Ben's aim was atrocious, the gun's range wasn't sufficient to reach a window – and it usually jammed. The weapon was confiscated by Uncle Mendel when Ben began firing at the local pigeons, his explanation that they might be carrying messages to the Germans not considered to be sufficient excuse for a bayonet charge down Zanzibar Terrace against one of them, which resulted in Ben tripping over a cobblestone, squeezing the trigger of his rifle as he went down, and the pellet freakishly ricocheting off the road to lodge in the lobe of his left ear. So it was back to the curtain rod.

As a further contribution to the War Effort, Ben decided to compile a list of potential enemy agents in the neighbourhood. He began with all the non-Jews he could think of, and was then at a loss as to how to continue – until, remembering something Mendel had said, he took his notebook and pencil to the baths one Friday night. Uncle Mendel was also there – and created a long-to-be-talked-about scene when, wearing only a towel, he dragged his equally half-naked (albeit steel-helmeted) brother into the street and proceeded to belabour him with strong words and weak fists.

'Not nice,' said my mother severely when told of the incident. 'Not nice. Shaming. You could end up in one of them Sunday papers.'

'It's not only under the armpits you got to look to see if someone's a real Jew,' Ben explained.

'Nearly got us all arrested,' Mendel muttered.

'And even them you think is Jewish needn't be,' Ben added. 'Like you yourself said: people pretend . . . They should be tested by the rabbi.'

'Tested?' his brother demanded. 'What does that mean?'

'You know: the Bible. Hebrew. Prayers. Talmud.'

Granny Abrams gave a hollow laugh. 'Half the Jews in England wouldn't pass such a test. So what you want they should do: shoot them?'

'You got to be on the safe side,' Ben rejoined. '*Bang! Bang!*' He winked and whistled a few bars of 'Run, Rabbit, Run.'

My mother clicked her teeth. Firmly: 'If this invasion means you're going to get your name in them Sunday papers, then it's better them Germans never come at all.' She emphasized this with several nods, then said shyly: 'Lysol, Mendel. You could do a roaring trade.' After a questioning grunt from her brother: 'I been thinking about it. I'd've mentioned earlier if it wasn't for this other business at the baths.' After a withering look at Ben: 'So there's this death-ray machine you was talking about that you've seen in black and white. But . . . well . . . just suppose, for the sake of argument, that them lowlifes do come marching up the street. OK, despite the arthritis and bunions and palpitations and aggravations, I'll also have a try with one of them bayonets. After all—'

'All you got to remember is four places,' said Ben. Illustrating with an imaginary weapon: 'Left breast . . . Right breast . . . Throat . . . Belly.'

My mother shuddered. 'Thank you very much. Just the same, Mendel, everybody might still need Lysol.'

Mendel frowned. 'You mean that having stabbed them to death we then maybe clean the wounds?'

An impatient '*Aaach!* . . . To drink. Kill ourselves with. If the Germans come (God forbid) then in the East End – all over – people will want to do away with themselves (may it never happen here). They say the gas oven's the most reliable – I read in the paper only the other day that thousands of people have done it very successful that way – but what if you haven't got a shilling handy for the meter? Or if you happen to be in the middle of Itchy Park or up The Lane? Where's there a gas oven? Does it stand to reason? And even if there is, so there's more queuing, and with mine arthritis it won't be a picnic I can tell you.

'Likewise the river, which I read is also very fashionable (although I can't say I fancy it with all them things floating). But how do you throw yourself in the river if you're miles away in Mare Street? You know what it's like waiting for a bus these days. You could starve to death before one comes to take you to the river. But a bottle Lysol everyone can have handy in the pocket. So while it's not for me to tell you what to do – after all, who's the business genus if not you? – just the same it's worth thinking about.'

As Uncle Mendel thought about it, Ben switched on the radio to hear the news broadcast. As the National Anthem was played he stood rigidly to attention (as always), then rebuked the rest of us (as always) for not doing likewise. My mother grimaced. 'When they get Al Jolson to sing it, I'll stand. In the meantime do me a favour and let's hear what's what.'

As far as she was concerned, the most dramatic item in the bulletin was an appeal for scrap metal, including bedsteads and pots and pans, which could be reprocessed into armaments. After a thoughtful pause: 'So all right – I'll sleep on the floor. I've got pains in my back I wouldn't wish on my worst enemy – but I'll sleep on the floor. But – but the pots and pans?' Her voice rose in shrill fury. 'OK, we've got nothing to cook because of this rotten rationing. But suppose, for the sake of argument, we did have something? A proper portion bones, or from a decent piece of stewing steak, or a halibut. What then? . . . Unless . . .' She inhaled sharply. 'Unless they argue that if we don't have no pots and pans we don't need no rations neither.' She brought her fist down on the table. 'Is that it, eh? Is that their dirty game? Because otherwise, if they want pots and pans why don't they do like everyone else and go buy from Timothy White's? So forget about the Lysol, Mendel: before the death rays or the bayonets we'll have starved to death.'

There was also an item in the news saying that an extra filter was to be fitted to all civilian gas masks in case the enemy used arsine gas – a statement that caused Uncle Mendel to roar triumphantly: 'See? Them Germans are so hard-up they'll use anything.'

Early one evening there was a knock at the door. After my mother had answered it, she called up the stairs: 'Simey! Come quick. There's a man.'

As I reached the door the visitor said: 'May I come in?' My mother replied: 'What's your business? If it's money you're after, my brother's away on business, and the other one's very high-up in the ARP.' To me: 'He's got some piece of paper, but I haven't got my glasses . . . So don't just stand there: read.'

I read. The man's card said that he represented the National Institution of Economic and Social Research.

'So what does that mean when it's at home?' my mother demanded.

'I'd like to ask you a few questions, madam.'

My mother shrugged. 'So ask. I might not answer, but like I tell this one, how will you learn if you don't ask?' She spread her hands. 'So ask.'

He opened his briefcase, took from it a clipboard to which was attached a pad of forms printed on the khaki paper of the day, delicately selected one of half-a-dozen pens in his breast pocket, unscrewed its cap, cleared his throat and asked: 'Would you object to taking your main meal in a canteen, madam?'

Automatically, my mother's first reaction was: 'Who's doing the cooking?' Then, frowning: 'Canteens? What's with canteens? You mean like them soup places up the road full of them Chinese and blackie sailors? Or like I remember my mother talking about when she first come off the boat from Poland? 'Cause if so, why?'

'No, madam. It's just to eke out the rations, the Government feels that it would help if people were prepared to eat in canteens.'

'You mean I got to take my rations there?'

A patient: 'No, madam. This would be on top of the rations.'

My mother, suspiciously: 'For one thing, what's with calling me "madam"? People who do that is usually after something. On top of which you offer food off the ration. How come? Why? Explain yourself. F'rinstance, what food? Is it Kosher? Is it, say f'rinstance, smoked salmon? Calves' liver? Barley soup? 'Cause if it is, that I can cook myself, so instead of mixing with people from God alone knows where, I can cook here at home. So don't bother with no canteens. Deliver here direct.' She nodded. 'You got a pen, so start writing. I want from ten pounds marrow bones, two pounds—'

'You don't understand, madam,' said the man, plainly harassed.

'I understand all right,' my mother retorted. 'Instead of going to kill Hitler (may his guts freeze) the Government sends madmen round with questions. Just say: am I going to get more bones or not?'

'Not in so many words, madam, but tell me: are you prepared to eat in a canteen?'

'Why should people eat in them all of a sudden?'

'It's not really . . . um . . . all of a sudden. There have been precedents for it.'

'I don't care if there been kings and queens for it – if you can give me extra in the canteen, why not in my own home? Not that it is my own home,' she added mournfully, 'except temp'ry.'

'Let's go on to the second question,' said the man desperately. 'Which newspapers do you read?'

'The answer will also kill Hitler?'

'It would be helpful to know, madam.'

'I read them all,' said my mother emphatically. 'No one reads more papers than me. Ask from the butcher, the fishmonger, the greengrocer (may they be constipated for life).'

'All?' Eyebrows raised, he studied his list. '*The Times? Manchester Guardian? Daily Telegraph?*'

A contemptuous: 'I mean real newspapers. Like the *Daily Mirror*, *Herald*, *Chronicle*, *Mail*, *The Star*, *News*, *Standard*. On Sundays the *Pictorial*, *News of the World* – you know, whatever I can get wrapped in.'

'Yes, yes, yes,' said the man quickly. 'Now

for the third question: do you follow the Ministry of Food hints in these papers?'

'Ministry of Food? Ministry of No Food, more like.' Her brow furrowed. 'And what's with hints? . . . Hints yet!' Her voice progressively rising to a shrill scream: 'You insinuating I need hints how to cook? So all right, these days there isn't any food, but are you saying I don't know how to cook it? You should be ashamed of yourself! You should have your mouth washed out in carbolic and beaten black and blue. How dare you say such things, you . . . you Fascist . . . And that's another thing: how do I know you're not a lousy rotten German with all them questions? Eh? Answer! Say! Show me your armpits. Where's Ben? . . . *Aie*, that madman's never here when you want him.'

Jabbing me in the chest with her elbow: 'Don't just stand there – go fetch a bayonet.' As the man began to retreat: 'You're not getting away so easy, you hooligan. Stay still while my baby goes run a message.' When the unfortunate man turned and began walking rapidly towards Cable Street, my mother raised her hands and her head and demanded of God: 'Why is there never a bayonet here when I need one?' As she lowered her head, a mighty '*Ah-ha!*' She took a rolled umbrella from the hallstand, and as the man broke into a trot she lurched after him shouting: 'Bosom! . . . Throat! . . . Guts! . . . Belly! . . . Keep still, you swine, while I do you a damage you'll never forget in a hurry . . .'

I closed the door, went to the kitchen and lit the gas under the soup. It was to take several bowls before my mother achieved some semblance of calm.

SEVEN

My mother flicked dust from the edge of my father's grave with a glove, slowly and painfully lowered herself to a sitting position, and used the glove to fan herself. '*Ach* but it's hot today . . . I must get my breath back . . . Like you know, this weather gives me palpitations, and it doesn't do my bunions no good neither, with all the walking.' She eased her feet from her shoes, wriggled her toes, gave a little sigh of pleasure, then flapped her gloves in my direction and said: 'Hop it.'

I moved away, but it was indeed too hot to walk far. I saw that Abraham Tulip's headstone had not been replaced or repaired, but it had fragmented in a manner that still made it possible to read the carved assurance that he would be remembered and mourned to all eternity. Near the grave was a tree. I squatted in its shade.

'. . . so here I am. September again. Times flies, eh? Except it's been a long year. No, things aren't easy, but I don't suppose they're no bed of roses for you, neither, may you rest in peace. The *vershtinkener* Germans are just across the Channel, but Mendel says we got a cigar box. Not that I mistrust him, but just the same . . .' (I could picture her looking guiltily over her shoulder) '. . . if this cigar box is all they say it is, why the rationing and shortages and all the youngsters in the family being called up? . . . The rationing's the worst. But we manage.

'The kids are all right, God be thanked. Ruthie's in the part-time Red Cross, mixing with a very nice class of doctor; Simey, when he's not driving me potty (he's here today, by the way, to say the prayer) runs messages in the blackout. Only he hasn't run none yet, so God alone knows what dirty work he gets up to. Mendel still buys and sells and dreams of America . . . America.' (I could visualize the shrug.) 'Still, if Jews didn't have dreams, what would they have? . . . Ben's still Ben, and Zillah is more aggravation than a tight corset, but at least I'm spared the heartburn from her cooking. (On top of everything else, that's all I'm short of.)

'As for Mother . . . well, she gets no younger (who does?) and while we all want she should live to be a hundred-and-twenty, nobody lasts for ever.' She clicked her teeth. '*Aie, aie, aie*, but I don't know why I'm so depressed today: there's time enough to worry when the time comes . . . So what have I got to cheer you up?

'Well, Rae's daughter, Selma, is getting married. You remember my sister, Rae, former Rachael? Selma's a nice girl. Nothing to write home about, but genuine.' A laugh. 'She reminds me of what you once said about Aaron's girl: she cooks like her mother, but looks like her father. Remember? Me, I remember like yesterday: we was on the charabanc outing to Higham's Park at the time. So anyway, for a girl who's no oil painting to marry the son from a wholesale maker of handbag straps is a good catch, no? He's called Tzuddik. Andrew Tzuddik (though why call a Yiddisher boy after salts for the liver I'll never understand. Unless he was previous also Aaron.) Anyway, I gave him a good talking-to. Made clear he was marrying into a good family, respected left, right and centre throughout the East End. Never a breath of scandal . . . unless you count one or two things people blew out of proportion. You know how excited some people get over nothing.

'He's a nice boy, and he's only got one eye God be thanked, so he can't go in the Army. He's with the family business but wants to start up on his own in the wireless after the war. Says he's got ambitions . . . Ambitions! . . . Like I've said a thousand times from the Yiddish: ambitions is what you want, old is what you get.

'Mind you, this is no time for a wedding. I told him straight, eyeball to eyeball. Not so much because of the war, 'cause if Jews waited for a time when there was no trouble they'd never marry. What I mean is that a wedding should be a wedding. Reception followed by a proper seven-, eight-course dinner. But these days with the rations, with the Government doing the lousy Germans' dirty work by starving us to death, who can have a proper Jewish wedding?

'So OK, there's extra rations for up to forty people. Forty people! At a wedding! Did you ever hear the like? You get more than that at a burial', adding, from force of habit, 'May it never happen here. And even for forty they don't allow enough for four. A teeny bit more sugar, a drop more milk . . . *Ach*, don't talk about it. Sure fish isn't rationed, but when was the last time anyone saw a salmon or Dover sole or a decent middle halibut?

'And the wedding cake! *Oi veh!* . . . You remember ours? Four, five feet tall. Seven, eight tiers, needed a special pantechnicon to carry. But these days? Don't ask. You're allowed a cake like a sixpenny sponge, and you borrow from the baker a cardboard cover to put over the top to make it look real. Did you ever hear such rubbish? Cardboard! Mind you, even at the best of times shop cakes can taste like cardboard (even home made, except this isn't the place to mention names). But these you don't only not eat, you also got to give back. So who's to know what toerags, what Tom, Dick and Harry, with God alone knows what diseases, have already borrowed, even if it is a Kosher baker?

'Ben did say he'd make one special out of an old hat box, but Selma didn't fancy. Ben means well, but sometimes the best favour he can do you is not do you a favour . . . And another thing I don't like: they're not marrying in a proper synagogue. Not a Register Office or a church, God forbid' (I heard her spit three times to ward off the evil eye) 'but almost as bad. In the Liberal Synagogue. Remember: them places where they have most of the service in English? Since when has God spoken English all of a sudden? Eh? Rae's Jakie must be turning in his grave 'til he's dizzy . . .'

Twenty minutes later, her passion temporarily spent, I was summoned to recite the memorial prayer, and we made our weary way from the cemetery in East Ham's Marlow Road back to Zanzibar Terrace.

Hot, dusty and aching, my mother put on the kettle to make tea for ourselves and Granny Abrams, the only other person at home when we arrived. 'Perhaps Simey could take chairs and a box into the street,' my grandmother suggested. 'It's like an oven in here.' I did so, and we drank our tea and ate strudel.

'A lovely day,' called a passing neighbour.

'You want a cup of tea?' my mother yelled.

'No time. The old man'll be home soon. Got to start cooking. He'll create ructions if it isn't ready on time.'

'Be grateful you got a husband,' my mother responded bitterly. To Granny Abrams: 'Even if he is a drunkard . . . You ready for a second cup?'

But at that moment there began a mournful wailing from across the roofs that slowly rose and fell in pitch and volume: air raid sirens sounding the Alert. With a scream of shock my mother dropped the teapot. It bounced from the orange box that served as our table and shattered on the pavement, splashing hot tea. A further scream, then an outraged: 'Now look what they made me do, the dog's-bodies. What they think they're playing at, frightening the life out of me like that? Can't they give some warning there's going to be a warning? And what's it this time? Another false alarm? More practice?' She raised her head to the grit-filtered blue of the London sky. 'You suppose teapots grow on trees? So haven't I got enough aggravations without teapots? What You got against me? Just say.'

The unnerving answer was a measured rat-tat-tat on plangent celestial kettledrums.

With a tremulous cry my mother went on her knees. Looking up at me, a quavering: 'W-what's He say? You been *bar mitzvah*'d, so you know Hebrew. Explain. Tell.'

I swallowed. 'Mum . . . that . . . that wasn't God. It was—'

She groaned. 'I knew it was too good to be true. With my luck I should have known better.' As she rose laboriously to her feet: 'So what was it?'

'Anti-aircraft guns. I – I think it's a real air raid.'

A shrill '*Oi gevult!*' Then: 'What's to be done? What's to become of us all?'

‘We can go to the air raid shelter at the corner,’ I suggested.

Granny Abrams, who’d been sitting bemused since the dropping of the teapot: ‘I’m going inside to have a lie down.’

‘But the bombs!’ my mother cried.

Granny Abrams shrugged. ‘If God wants me, where better to find me than in my own bed? And if He doesn’t?’ Another shrug.

When I said that we could go to the cellar, my mother pursed her lips. ‘I don’t fancy it, but Ben said he got prepared – and anything’s better than standing out here.’ As the anti-aircraft fire intensified: ‘Hurry! Help your grandmother. The cups and saucers and chairs can wait.’

In the feeble light of the cellar’s solitary dust- and flyspecked bulb we saw that Ben’s preparations had consisted solely of pasting-up various Ministry of Information propaganda posters. Our furniture was at one end of the cellar, covered in the Edward the Eighth decorated oilcloth, while much of the remaining space was occupied by piles of sand, items of Uncle Mendel’s stock (mysterious heaps and bundles and tea chests identifiable only as silhouettes) and the home-made forge on which Ben made his bayonets.

‘It’s years since I been down here,’ said Granny Abrams as she sat on the edge of a tea chest. ‘Smells damp.’

'You're right,' my mother agreed as she lowered herself gingerly onto another chest. 'It's not going to do my—' She was interrupted by a shrill whistling sound followed, after a second's pause, by a rumbling series of explosions that caused the house above us to tremble. 'W-was that the b-bombs?' she asked in a small voice. When I nodded she added, almost as a plea: 'Does that mean it's over?'

'I doubt it,' I replied, and was right. For that evening, September 17, marked the start of the London Blitz. The Germans' target: the dockland of the East End.

The hours that followed remain even now a chaos of fragmented recall . . . The horror of what soon became an incessant lunacy of mind-bending and deafening noise – planes, bombs, guns, crashing masonry and the bells of Civil Defence vehicles combined in an idiot cacophony of terror . . . The sickening feeling that the house did not collapse under the reverberation of exploding bombs only because it was held together by its neighbours . . . Above all, the indescribable torture of sitting helpless, every bomb a screaming eternity of rib-thumping fear as we awaited its explosion.

My mother's shoulders shook as she sat weeping, her head in her hands, her breath coming in agonized gasps. Granny Abrams, outwardly at least, seemed relatively calm. Lined and tired and old, she nodded to herself as her lips moved in what I supposed to be prayer. At some point my mother blinked away and sniffed away her tears and asked: 'Y-you all right, Mother?'

Granny Abrams sighed. Wearily in Yiddish: 'I've endured over eighty years' anti-semitism, pogroms, Cossacks and deaths, so what's one more of God's jokes? Eh? No, don't worry from me, it's the others you should worry for.'

'You think I don't?' my mother howled, again bursting into tears. Between sobs: 'Ruthie, Mendel, Ben, Herschel . . .' Having recited the names of not only those members of the family who resided at Zanzibar Terrace, but those who lived across the sprawl of the East End, an anguished: 'How are they? Where are they? Are they all in one piece? . . . I came from Kilburn so we'd be together. So I'd know what was happening. But I still don't know from nothing . . .' A *pshaw* of a laugh. 'Cigar boxes, yet!'

There was the moment when my mother gasped and demanded: 'Where's Itchky?'

'I don't know,' I replied. 'Probably upstairs somewhere, asleep.'

'Asleep!' my mother yelled, momentarily back to normal. 'With all this going on? It's not natural. He's out more like, getting himself bombed to death when he should be here doing his duty, watching for mice. It's that vet I blame, that Jacobson, for not doctoring him proper. Why else go rushing out like a maniac in the bombing?' A shrill scream. 'And this cellar is probably alive with mice, rats, and Heaven above knows what else. I read in the paper . . . Simey, go bang on the floor.'

'There's isn't enough noise?' I asked.

'That's up there. I'm talking from down here. Go bang.'

As I rose to my feet Granny Abrams patted my mother's hand. 'Leave be.'

'If you want to give this assassin right, give him right,' said my mother sulkily. 'If you want we should be eaten alive, OK, we'll be—' She broke off with a shriek as an explosion close by caused plaster to fall from the ceiling.

At some point I realized that our furniture heaped at the end of the cellar contained chairs. I fetched three, and rummaging produced cushions . . .

There's the memory of my own shocked cry as I realized that I should have been on duty at the Air Raid Wardens' Post.

'In the bombing!' my mother screamed. 'You gone mad or something?'

'When else should I run messages?' I demanded.

'If the phones are bombed, they'll stay bombed, you *dumkopf*. They'll still be bombed when this' (she flapped her hands towards the ceiling) 'is over and done with. So then run the messages.' A lightning change of mood brought weary resignation. 'I haven't got the strength to argue. So go. Run. Do what you think best. You're a big boy. Don't worry about me. I'll manage. Don't worry from your grandmother, neither. If we get buried alive we'll manage, eh Mother? It's not enough we got the others to worry about, we now got this Count Potocki of a Cossack to add to the list . . . So don't stand there – run. Go enjoy yourself.' Voice rising: 'But you mark my words: you'll be sorry the way you're treating me. You'll rue the day. When you're out there, blown to smithereens, you'll regret for the rest of your life the way you treated your own mother. And if we also get bombed to Timbuctoo, why should you worry? So go have pleasure. Go about your dirty work . . .'

I stayed.

Another memory from the chaos of that day: my mother's horrified: 'The soup! The gas masks! Where's the carrier bags?'

I, too, had forgotten our survival kits.

'They're in the hall. But I don't know about Granny's.'

'Don't know? What you mean, don't know? It's not enough your own mother should be starved and gassed to death (and for my part I don't care: I'm used to such things) but your grandmother? That saint among women? You should have your mouth washed out in disinfectant – which, come to think of it, is also in the carrier bags.' To Granny Abrams: 'Where's your gas mask and things?'

Granny Abrams shrugged. 'Maybe the kitchen. Maybe the bedroom.'

'I'll go and look,' I said.

'Don't you dare move!' my mother shrilled. 'You don't know what might be going on up there. I'll go.'

'Don't be silly. I'll be much quicker than you.'

'No! Stay where you are.'

'What about the soup?'

'We'll do without.'

'What about Granny Abrams?'

A wail. 'That's also true.'

My grandmother: 'Don't worry from me. Anyway, I'm not hungry.'

'But you must eat something. I read only the other day, so sure I should live, that it's very dangerous to get bombed on an empty stomach. I swear—'

I scuttled up the stairs, found Granny Abrams' gas mask in her bedroom, but no emergency carrier bag. I collected ours, and for good measure searched for Itchky. I found him asleep under the kitchen table wheezingly oblivious of the death and destruction about him. 'Come and save us from the mice,' I said as I scooped him under one arm. His response was a resentful spit and claw strikes on my hands that took the best part of a month to heal.

As I clattered back to the cellar, my mother's quavering: 'You all right?'

'I'm fine,' I assured her. 'And the house seems all right, too – as far as I can make out. But with the windows open the place is smothered in dust.'

My mother shook a fist towards the ceiling. 'The rotters! Toerags! Killers! They haven't done enough damage already without dust? May . . . may . . .' She finally found a suitable malediction. 'May their children break their legs when they dance on their graves.'

'Why the excitement?' asked my grandmother. 'Zillah does the dusting.'

'Not my room she doesn't,' said my mother firmly. 'That I do myself. Or Ruth, when she hasn't got her nose buried in some rubbishy book. Anyway, what about the food? It's not enough the muck you get these days tastes like dust and ashes, you also want . . .' She broke off with a frown. After a shrug, she unscrewed the top from a vacuum flask. 'Here Mother, have some soup while it's hot . . . Thank God the others have got their carrier bags.' The tears came again as she added in a whisper: 'If they're alive to eat it . . .'

At last the All Clear. Physically and emotionally exhausted, we made our way upstairs: Granny Abrams to put on the kettle, my mother and I to look outside.

It was an awesome sight. Through a brown-grey curtain of dust I saw that while Zanzibar Terrace had apparently survived the raid without damage, we were circled by a black-streaked curtain of dull crimson as great areas of the docks and the City burned, while the sky above us was hidden by a swirling cloud of smoke.

Slowly others came from their homes to gather in small groups on the shrapnel-littered road and pavements. I thought my mother would want to join them, but she stood in rocking silence, biting her lower lip. Finally a sigh as she threw up her hands in a gesture of weary despair and turned to go back into the house. We then saw that our cups and saucers were fragmented on the pavement, and that the seat of a chair was transfixed with a sliver of grey metal. 'Chairs they're welcome to,' said my mother flatly, and went to the kitchen.

Aunt Zillah was the first to arrive home, welcomed by embraces and the tearful, near-hysteric relief that was to greet the rest of the family. She had been visiting a sister when the Alert sounded, and they'd taken refuge in an official shelter constructed in the basement of a neighbouring bakery. The tale she told had much in common with ours, but the true magnitude of events began to emerge when she described her journey home: a trembling-voiced account of the morning's homes and shops and business premises now smouldering rubble, and of rescue workers tearing at the ruins in the hope of finding life beneath them. 'And I only got a glimpse,' she assured us. 'A glimpse. Because I had to come round miles out of the way, so much is blocked-off by the bombing and the police.'

Then Mendel staggered in with a story which added grim emphasis to the appalling picture. 'The whole area's a ruin,' he concluded.

'The dirty dogs,' said my mother flatly. 'With the whole of London to bomb, why the East End? Because it's full of Jews, that's why. And not only Jews: the poor Jews. So if that rotten Hitler must bomb Yiddisher people (may his daughters marry gypsies) why not the Jews from Golders Green and Finchley and them other places? People who can afford to be bombed?'

'Where were you when the siren went?' Zillah asked him.

Mendel raised his head and gave a wry smile. 'Where was I? I'd just come out of synagogue. That's where I was. Eyeball to eyeball with Fleischmann. About to do a deal that would have fetched me a fortune. A fortune,' he repeated – but the thunder was missing. When he went on to say 'Seeds' it was without his usual roar of triumph, and 'It came to me like that' was accompanied by only a token finger-snap.

It was clear that Mendel's heart wasn't in the story – as though he continued it rather than have to sit and think of Ben and Herschel, Ruth and Sybil. For the same reason we forced ourselves to listen. '. . . You follow? All over there's a shortage food. But there's also places for people to grow. Gardens. Fields. In the parks. Everywhere. But how can you grow food without seed? Like it says in the Bible: "From the seed of the whatsit". Eh? It stands to reason, no? And then Fleischmann mentions these seeds he bought years ago but forgot about. In fact he's had so long he's even forgot what's in the sack: corn, barley, wheat, grits, butter beans, flour. He doesn't know. So all he wants is to get rid of . . . Get rid of! May God blind me for life: get rid of! Mad, huh? Because you know something? If I had a park or a garden or even a farm I'd make a million. May my mice die of hunger if I lie: a million.

'Like in that picture with Jack Holt and the girl in the leather skirt. From just one bag seeds – one bag! – they grew corn you could see for hundreds of miles. What am I saying? Hundreds? *Thousands!*' He was near-excited for a few seconds. 'From one bag of seeds. Even their children ended up with motor cars and changed their clothes three times a day while the music played.' Slumping with tiredness: 'But where can I grow anything?'

Granny Abrams: 'Don't I remember we got a flowerpot out the back somewhere? One of the grandchildren gave for mine birthday with a flower in. So take. Go grow.'

As Uncle Mendel ground his teeth my mother said: 'I'm so tired I don't know if I'm coming or going. But just say – if you haven't got no fields, no leather skirts, what's with seeds?'

'Because like I said, other people can grow . . . But then the bloody air raid siren went and while I went to the cellar under the synagogue with the rabbi and everybody else, Fleischmann has a stroke. Just my luck, eh?'

Having whistled their astonishment and sympathy, my mother said: 'What a shocking thing, may it never happen here,' and Aunt Zillah said, uncharacteristically mollifying: 'Maybe it wouldn't have been such a bargain, Mendel. If Fleischmann forgot what seeds they were, suppose they was bird seed?'

Mendel patted his boils as he considered this. With a yawn: 'Maybe you're right . . . though even then they'd be useful to help grow more chickens. For isn't chickens also birds? . . . But what does it matter? What does anything matter?'

Next to come were Ruth and Sybil, almost asleep on their feet, with hardly coherent accounts of chaotic attempts by their undermanned First Aid Post to cope with an emergency situation that had arisen on a scale no one had thought possible.

Ben. His clothes were almost in shreds. His hands, clutching a number of carrier bags, were clumsily bandaged with strips of bloodstained cloth. He interrupted the Babel of questions with a hoarse: '*Ssssh*, I'll tell you . . . I was on my way to the shelter just as Levy the butcher got bombed.' When the gasps had subsided he raised his hands and nodded at them. 'I helped dig out. Levy and the family were all right, thank God, but the shop and the upstairs had gone. So he said to take what I like. A . . . a thank you. I said I didn't want nothing—'

An automatic reflex of a scream from my mother. 'Nothing? From a butcher you'd take nothing? *Oi veh!*'

Ben managed a smile. 'He then said it wasn't no good to him no more, so I took. I know you like bones Minnie, so in one of them carriers is all I could manage to get in. In the others is a couple chickens and meat. I don't know from what sort.' He again indicated his hands. 'I couldn't carry no more, and I didn't have the barrow . . . But we'll have some of your *lockshen* soup, eh?'

'Soup?' my mother cried. 'Of course soup. What else? . . . But the hands. First the hands. Come to the sink and wash. Ruth! Sybil! You're in the Cross so go fetch Lysol, iodine, carbolic. And fresh cloths to bandage with. Then soup. So sure I should live, there's nothing better for the hands than soup. Builds the blood . . . *Oi gevult*, the blood! Come quick and wash.' As she ran the tap and Ben peeled off the rags around his hands: 'Soup. Naturally soup. What else to build the blood? But hands is also important, so you got somewhere to put the blood into . . .'

Finally Herschel arrived, eyes bloodshot, hands, face and uniform black with soot. He did not reply to the clamour of questions, but laboriously climbed the stairs to his bedroom. Later Mendel went up and undressed him as he slept, then Zillah took a bowl of water, soap and a towel and washed him.

The rest of us could now go to our beds, even though there were nagging worries about other members of the family. As her daughter and daughter-in-law helped her up the stairs, Granny Abrams asked hopefully: 'So that's it? It's over?'

'I wouldn't be so sure,' Aunt Zillah replied.

She was right, of course. Eight months were to pass before we knew another peaceful night.

Like millions of others, we came to accept the Blitz as an integral part of daily life. But first there was the problem of deciding how best to protect ourselves.

Mendel: 'What about the shelter at the corner? It's been done up proper. Real nice. Cosy. Even painted. So sure I should live to see my children married: painted. Under Solly Litvak the furrier's place. The King of England don't do no better. By my life – the King.'

'You could be right,' said Aunt Zillah. 'And it'll also be the nearest I'll ever get to a fur coat.'

'I seen it,' said Ben. 'Full of wooden bunks to sleep. Steel girders to keep up the ceiling. Sandbags. Like in the First War.'

My mother screamed. 'First War?! I heard you talk enough from the First War! Them trenches with the lice and rats and tinned jam and mud up to the armpits you talked about. They wanted to build the same in Kilburn 'til I got the mayor to put the lid on it. And that's where you want we should sleep at night? Thank you very much! I'd rather take my chances here. All right, so being bombed to death is nothing to write home about, but I've also got to sit up to here in mud?'

'No, Minnie,' said Ben. 'I wasn't talking about the trenches. When we was in reserve.'

'So go reserve for someone else. And who's to know what toerags you find there? Drunkards. Lowlifes. No-goods. People with the phlegm. People with . . .' She wriggled uncomfortably '. . . well, with thoughts on the brain.'

'It's not like that,' said Mendel. 'I got it on good authority from Solly Litvak himself who was down there personal. He said that once they got used to it, it was singing and dancing and joking. Like . . . like a party.'

My mother frowned. 'Party?'

'Sure a party,' said Mendel eagerly. 'May God strike me down dead and then give me gumboils – a party.'

My mother gave a dismissive shrug. 'All the more reason not to go – I got nothing to wear . . . And another thing: is there a special room for women? Cause I don't feel like sleeping with no strange men with the phlegm. Nor women, come to that. It can be very dangerous crowded together. One person with a disease and it spreads like wildfire. I read in black and white in the paper only the other day that it's happened in London before.'

When questioning revealed that she was referring to a story she'd read about the Great Plague, and when I pointed out that this had occurred nearly three hundred years earlier, she hurled a handful of radishes at me. 'So it can't happen again, clever Dick? You only ever had one cold in your life? One chilblain? One headache? Eh? So why only one plague? So like I say: is this place fumigated regular? And is the bedding clean?'

'You take your own,' Mendel told her.

A long '*Mmmmm*' as my mother considered this. 'Suppose it gets stolen? Parties or no parties, these places must attract all the ruffians from kingdom-come.'

'You take it with you every night and bring it back in the morning,' Mendel explained wearily.

My mother shook her head. 'I don't fancy. Having to make a poppy show with my sheets and blankets. Also, how are we supposed to manage everything? Cause there's also the *perrener*. With mine arthritis and bunions and palpitations and other aggravations, I'm also expected to *shlep* all that back and forward every time the siren goes? . . . And what about my few bits and pieces in the American trunk? My best corset, the photos, Nathan's things – and all the rest. I'm supposed to let them get bombed to Timbuctoo while I'm at this party? On top of which there's the carrier bags.' A triumphant: '*Ah-ha*! What about Mother? She's also expected to fetch and carry?'

'I'll take the things on the barrow,' said Uncle Ben. 'Take early when it's still light and before I go on duty.'

'What duty?' asked his brother suspiciously.

Uncle Ben gave an elaborate wink. 'Walls Have Ears. Top Secret.'

As Uncle Mendel gave a contemptuous splutter, Granny Abrams said: 'What about the lav? . . . What sort of lavs they got in them shelters?'

Mendel shrugged. 'I haven't had time to

inspect. I'll ask from Solly Litvak.'

Ben shook his head. 'There aren't none. No plumbing.'

'That's that then,' said my mother firmly. 'That puts the lid on it. The very idea! On top of everything else to have to carry chambers pots to and fro. Just imagine: hundreds of people in the shelter with pots. I must say, Mendel, you may be the family genus, but you got a very funny idea about parties.'

'I wasn't going to go anyway,' said Granny Abrams. 'I asked just for the sake from curiosity.'

Aunt Zillah: 'So what we going to do?'

'We should have got them Anderson Shelters when they was offered,' said Ben. 'They went to anyone earning under two hundred and fifty pounds a year.'

'Under?' my mother exclaimed. 'Under? Who earns over? So go fetch.'

'He's talking rubbish. As per usual,' said Uncle Mendel. 'You got to dig a hole to put them in. What was it – eight feet long, six feet wide, five feet deep? Something like that. So where am I going to dig such a hole? The cellar? And if I did, how can we all get in it? Is it logic? Does it stand to reason?'

'These days nothing stands to reason,' said my mother with feeling.

Granny Abrams thoughtfully: 'The cellar . . . Ben, wasn't you supposed to do things?' As my uncle shuffled his feet and plucked at the flowers on the wallpaper: 'So these steel things. I don't understand nothing from nothing, but if Litvak can do it, why not us? Only without strangers. Just family. Eh? Because so sure I should live, I'm not going to no shelter.'

The firmness of this last statement leaving no room for argument, Mendel nodded and said: 'So we got to organize the cellar. Tomorrow, cabbage head, go get girders.'

Ben blinked at him. 'From where am I supposed to get girders?'

His brother bared his teeth and shook his fists. 'I haven't enough to do already, without having to worry about every tuppeny-ha'penny problem that crops up? In America I'd only have to give a nod and a wink' (he demonstrated) 'and the tickle tapes'd start tickling, and before you can say how's your father I'd have enough iron girders to build another of them Eyefuls like they got in Paris.'

'I suppose you was misled by them dirty anti-semites again,' said my mother mournfully. 'Funny, eh? They locked Mosley up (God be thanked) but what's a prison if not full of steel and iron? He's probably safe as houses. Better off than any of us.'

Uncle Mendel frowned at her. 'So how was I misled?'

'Eh? . . . Oh, I was just thinking. All over the country there's cellars. Basements. People must be crying out for them iron girdles. So if you'd known in time you could also have nodded and winked and tickled and whatever. Now I suppose it's too late.'

There were to be no girders. But Ben did clumsily repair the bayonet holes in his coal sacks, fill them with sand and built a sort of blast carpet on that part of the yard which overlapped the cellar, leaving room for a path to the lavatory (a snaking passageway along which my mother was convinced that with her luck a bomb was certain to fall – if she hadn't already broken her neck negotiating it in the blackout).

Supervised by Uncle Mendel, the younger members of the household swept and scrubbed the cellar and Uncle Ben whitewashed it and ran dangerously improvised extensions from the light socket to increase illumination. Mendel's stock was neatly piled into a corner, and to help counter the damp Aunt Zillah brought her paraffin stove from the bedroom.

My mother, inspired: 'If we're going to be buried alive in the cellar every time the alarm goes, I got my sticks of furniture there. It could do with an airing. Maybe not all the furniture . . .' She shrugged away the ridiculousness of the idea. 'But some. A few tables. More chairs. The lino. The dresser. Sideboard. Maybe a few photos on the wall, vases and the sofa. Also—'

'Do you mind leaving just a bit of room?' asked Aunt Zillah.

'Sure,' said my mother generously. 'What you want to bring down?'

'A few human beings.'

'Eh?'

'By the time you've done up the place like Buckingham Palace where's there going to be room for us?'

'It's all right for you,' my mother snapped. 'You got a home. Me and my babies, we got nothing.' Voice rising: 'And you begrudge us even putting out a few bits and pieces in a cellar soaking wet with mice and rats.' Reaching a scream: 'May I never leave this room alive if I don't go straight down to that cellar and chop the furniture to firewood. May I have a black year if I don't. Then you'll have all the room you want. Simey! Go fetch from Herschel's axe. Ruth, get ready in case there's blood. Then we're packing our bags and moving out. I'd rather beg in the streets and sleep with them people with the phlegm than spend another minute where I know I'm not wanted. May God—'

'Enough already,' Granny Abrams commanded, slapping her hand on the table. '*Aie, aie, aie* . . . There's not enough fighting and arguing in the world outside? You also got to bring into the home? Like the Zuglischer Rabbi used to say, when Jews quarrel all their enemies join in the laughing.'

'Who's quarrelling?' asked Aunt Zillah hotly. 'All I said—'

'I know what you said,' my mother yelled. 'And I also know what I said. Don't worry: I'll be out of here before you can say Jack Robinson.'

My grandmother sighed. 'Minnie, do me a favour and put out the furniture. Simey'll give you a hand. So will Ben.'

'But I swore to God.'

Granny Abrams nodded her head and half-smiled. 'If God listened to all the swearing there'd be no Jews, no Christians, no Cossacks, no Hitlers, no nothing. So leave God alone for five minutes. He's got enough to do already. Go arrange from the furniture.'

We did, and although my mother had to agree, grudgingly, that there wasn't room for as much as she'd have liked, what we did put out indeed gave the cellar a bizarre semblance of cosiness.

Ben supplied the final touch. From his savings he purchased a battered old horn gramophone. 'For the records, Minnie,' he explained shyly. Since my mother was the only member of the household to possess records, and only two at that, the point came when the sounds of the air raids became near-preferable to the interminable playings of Al Jolson's 'Sonny Boy' (on the reverse side 'There's A Rainbow Round My Shoulder'), and Sophie Tucker's 'My Yiddisher Momma' (one side in English, the other in Yiddish).

Uncle Mendel was finally driven to negotiate a job lot of fifty second-hand gramophone records, of which forty were useless and the rest barely playable. One of the latter was Deanna Durbin singing 'Ave Maria' which, because of its appalling scratchiness, Uncle Mendel was convinced was a curiously foreign pronunciation of 'I've A Metsieh'. Since *metsieh* was Yiddish for bargain, Mendel adopted it as a sort of extra and recurrent evening psalm, and so we ended up with a sanity-threatening non-stop repeat repertoire of two-and-a-half records, for nobody ever discovered what was on the reverse side of the closely guarded Deanna Durbin.

EIGHT

It did not take my mother long to appreciate that the cellar could serve as a sort of salon where, circumstances permitting, she could entertain her friends during the daylight hours.

Not that she regarded it as entertaining. 'I'm ashamed. To have to offer a cup of tea like water. But what can you do when they give two ounces each a week? And not real tea neither. Dust. On top of that, grey bread. The baker says it's good for you. I told him straight, eyeball to eyeball, there are times when senna pods is also good for you. Maybe there are times when this rubbish is also good for you. But not when I want bread . . . If that wasn't enough, I can only give one biscuit each. It's true enough that Mrs Klopps offered to bring a cake she cooked. But if she brings you got to eat, and to be honest I'd rather do without. Dough like Plasticine.' A giggle. 'In a way a good thing. One bite and you spend the rest of the night chewing, so you don't eat more than a mouthful. She should go bake for the Government – be a big saving on the rationing . . . Maybe I can also give a tail haddock like a bone, and one choice herring. One choice! . . . And that's tea? You give more to a tramp begging in the gutter.'

Mrs Block spent her nights in the shelter under Solly Litvak's workshop, and although she swore that it was a friendly place with no signs of phlegm or thoughts on the brain, and not even a mention of chamber pots, I noticed that from then on my mother always provided her with the same cup, saucer and plate, and later washed and drained them separately from the others.

Mrs Krenk and Mrs Klopps took refuge in the flat of friends of Mrs Klopps: it was supposed that since the husband, a Mr Blintz, was a maker of fringes for ritual garments, the sacred quality of his profession would guarantee divine protection. When the flat was flooded after an unexploded incendiary bomb smashed through the roof tiles and water tank, the two women transferred to Aldgate underground station, from where Ada Krenk wrote nightly postcards to the Chief Rabbi urging him to have Mr Blintz's armpits examined, and that if only they could find her mislaid husband he'd get to the bottom of it all in no time at all.

Rosie Speck caused a sensation when she

announced that she was giving up dress-making to nurse an elderly cousin on her mother's side – a retired bookbinder and widower who lived in Hackney, thus obliging her to spend most of her nights as well as days away from home. 'It's his bowels, if you see what I mean,' she explained.

'I see what she means all right,' said my mother later. 'I see all right. Oh yes, I see, plain as day. For where's the bowels if not . . . Well, you know . . . Eh? . . . No point beating about the bush . . .' Lowering her voice: '*Very close to certain portions of the body.*'

Mrs Block: 'It's not nice messing about with strange men's bowels.'

'But it's her cousin she's nursing,' I protested. 'Not a stranger.'

My mother beat me about the head. 'How dare you contradict, you Fascist toerag? And how do we know she's got a cousin, eh girls? Since when a cousin? How come a cousin all of a sudden? Have any of you heard talk of a cousin? And a cousin with the bowels yet?'

Mrs Klopps: 'You got to admit that every-one's got bowels, Mrs Ashe.' Nodding her head: 'They come in very handy.'

'So you're taking her part,' my mother exploded.

Mrs Krenk, absently: 'Useful.'

Mrs Klopps: 'Didn't I just say?'

Mrs Krenk: 'I meant that with her being former a dressmaker before she took up with this nursing, she's handy with a needle and thread. Can come in useful.'

My mother frowned. 'I don't follow you.'

'To sew people up.'

Mrs Klopps: 'Why should she want to sew his bowels up?'

Before Mrs Krenk could reply, a long whistle of astonishment from my mother. 'You're right. It could be dangerous. Cause troubles all the Ex-Lax in the world wouldn't put a stop to . . . *Oi veh*, just to think that here she was, only yesterday, pretending to be a friend, and now she's going about sewing up the bowels. It should be put a stop to. Reported. I'll talk to my Ruthie who's very high-up in the Red Cross. She'll have a word with one of the doctors there.'

Mrs Block: 'Like Mrs Klopps said, why should she want to sew up?'

My mother: 'Why should she want to go to Hackney? Eh? Answer me that. If she wants to sew up the bowels, why not do it local? Why Hackney? . . . I'll tell you why. Because bookbinders must be rich men, no? Not as rich as butchers . . .' She shrugged away the absurdity of such a comparison '. . . but not short of a few thousand. That's why. And with her not married she'll be able to—' A knock at the front door interrupted her. 'Who can that be?' To me: 'So don't sit there like a stuffed monkey, go answer. If it's for money, say you're not in. If it's anything else, say to come back later when Mendel's home.'

The caller was Benny Begel, rheumy eyes blinking from a grizzled thicket of beard, his back bowed from a lifetime of carrying sacks of those hoops of Jewish-style rolls – begels – that earned him his nickname, and which he sold from street to street in and around the East End. His Yiddish was fluent, as was his knowledge of the local Jewish population, so he was employed part-time by the council to attempt to explain the latest Government laws, regulations and exhortations to those who could not read or fully understand English, and to make minor general inquiries.

'What's up?' I asked.

'You,' he replied. 'They want to know why you're not running the messages.'

Reluctant to say that my mother wouldn't let me, I temporized with: 'Top Secret. Walls Have Ears. Be Like Dad – Keep Mum.'

I was saved from further embarrassment by my mother's shrill: 'Who is it? If it's the landlord say we're all bombed to death.'

'It's Benny Begel.'

'He's got begels? Ask him in for a cup of tea.'

Benny Begel had no begels. 'With the shortage from the flour and fat and things I get a supply that goes in five minutes.' A harsh laugh. 'For the first time in forty years I don't have to *shlep* street to street and beg people to buy: they come running. Only I got nothing to sell. Funny, eh?'

'I'm in stitches,' said my mother flatly. 'And they're also grey, them begels you haven't got?'

'Grey?'

'The rubbishy flour.'

'*Aaaah*, grey . . .' Benny nodded. 'Grey all right. That's a fact. Like in what they call the National Loaf. Mind you, they say it's good for you. Supposed to help you lose weight.' He patted his stomach. 'Not that it's done me no good.'

'Maybe you don't eat enough,' my mother suggested. 'But if there's a shortage of begels, how you managing? With the weddings?'

At this reference to his sideline as a marriage broker, Benny Begel spluttered biscuit crumbs across the table. 'You must be joking, missus. The last time I arranged a marriage was . . . oh, I can't even remember the date. But years ago. Between the Klesmer boy – the one with the fits who was a barber in Club Row before he went in the Navy – and the Podeschwa girl with the hair.

'Weddings! In my father's day in *Der Heim* – the Old Country – everything was different.' As he licked crumbs from a fingertip: 'Mind you, fair's fair: it had to be different. With people in the villages, hundreds of miles from nowhere, it was only them what travelled – the pedlars, rabbis and what have yous – that met people with sons and daughters to be married. So the arrangements were made. Didn't your own mother tell me that's how she married your father? Didn't meet him 'til the engagement? All arranged by the parents? And didn't it work out? . . . Eh? . . . Eh? . . . Mmmm? . . . Believe me, in them days the parents were the guv'nors. And they knew. Wasn't your parents happy, Mrs Ashe?'

'Happy?' my mother exclaimed. 'Happy?' Tears filled her eyes. 'My mother (may she live to be a hundred-and-twenty), and my father (may he be sitting with mine Nathan on the left hand of God) was more happy than *lockshen* is with chicken soup.' Angrily: 'How can you compare?'

Benny Begel's forehead furrowed, his eyebrows lowering to join his beard so that only a purple button of nose was visible between cloth cap and collar stud. 'Compare? Who's comparing?'

'You are.'

'With who?'

'Anyone. Them saints among people . . . To-to – mention in the same breath. You should be ashamed. Have your mouth washed out.'

'Look missus, even the Chief Rabbi himself had his marriage arranged. The Chief Rabbi! So sure I'm sitting here, it was arranged. By my cousin, Maczinski the slaughterer, who was also a cousin on the mother's side to the Wonder Rabbi of Lodz.'

My mother clicked her teeth. 'A wonder rabbi in the family yet,' Quickly recovering: 'So what's that got to do with the price of begels?'

Mrs Krenk: 'What does that mean?'

My mother shrugged. 'How should I know? But everything means something. Even begels. It says in the Bible.'

Mrs Klopps: 'My husband – the one who was assistant caretaker from Fieldgate Street – never said nothing about begels.'

My mother, angrily: 'So now he knows more than the Bible, all of a sudden? More than God?'

Mrs Block quickly intervened with: 'To go back to the marriages, Benny. You was saying . . .?'

'Saying? I was saying that today there's nothing with nothing. Even just before the war there was some business, except it was more like a good deed. People was glad of a bit of help. People with the hair, the eyes, the legs – know what I mean? Today everyone's too independent. Them with the arms don't want with the lungs, and the legs don't want the pockmarks, the fits don't want the twitch, and the ones with the spine don't want the wind . . . *Aaach*, everybody knows better than the experts.' He looked speculatively round him. 'Now you ladies. Widows. Very nice ladies. What they call attractive. You want I should make a few inquiries? F'rinstance there's Rosen the Baker in Waterloo which is very close Mayfair. He—'

My mother, voice dangerously calm: 'What you insinuating? . . . Oi, if only my poor husband was alive.'

'But he isn't, missus,' said Benny Begel.

'Ah-ha! So now you're taking advantage of a defenceless widow. Is that it? 'Cause if so, you got a barefaced cheek.'

A movement of Benny's facial hair indicated a smile. 'Barefaced? With my beard?'

'Like they say in Yiddish,' my mother snorted, 'a goat has a beard, but that don't make him a rabbi.'

'That's true,' said Mrs Klopps. 'Now when my husband, may he rest in peace, was at Fieldgate Street, the rabbi there – Mordisch – had a beard down to his belly. Even my husband had one to his chest. But yours? It's hardly over the neck. Like the mange you got.'

'What about Rabbi Coppelstone from Mile End?' Mrs Block demanded. 'Beard down over the knees. Now that's what I call a real rabbi.'

'Him I also know,' said Benny Begel. 'A white beard, but a green brain.'

'Meaning what?' my mother demanded.

'Meaning like that Mrs Fisch, the refugee woman who come from Vienna before the war. Back in when was it? Thirty-three? Four? Anyhow, she got sent to Temple Road in East Ham – the one near the cemetery – when it should have been the Temple Road in Cricklewood. So she went to Coppelstone for help: to arrange a message to the other Temple Road.

'He says nothing is without meaning (like you was saying with the begels, Mrs Ashe).' As my mother smirked complacently: 'There must have been a reason God sent her to the East End instead from Cricklewood. But what reason? What was His will? Coppelstone started working out. And when he starts working out! *Oi veh!* What this Talmudic rabbi said, and that one said. On the one hand this, on the other that. And what was said in Zohar, the Books of Enoch and Ezra, the

Book of Brightness, the Book of—' He interrupted himself with: '*Pshaw!* . . . Everything contradicted everything else, so after five or six years she was still waiting from the answer.'

'Five, six years!' my mother exclaimed. 'Why not catch a bus? Cricklewood is no distance. Just up the road from where I was in Kilburn. From there, five minutes on the bus. From here – what? Twenty minutes? So all right, these days you got to wait for buses. But five, six years? Is it natural? Does it stand to reason? She so short of money for the fare? If so, I'll give personal.'

Benny Begel shook his head. 'She was a very religious lady – wouldn't do nothing without the rabbi's OK. Thought it'd be unlucky. So she waited.'

Mrs Block: 'For five, six years?'

Mrs Klopps: 'What happened?'

'What happened?' Benny sucked noisily at his tea. 'Don't ask what happened. She got killed when that bomb fell on Piler Flats in Holledge Street where she had a room with the Embersteins.'

My mother: 'What a shocking thing! And that . . . that was God's will?'

Benny Begel drily: 'Coppelstone's still working out . . . But you got to be fair, I suppose. Like it says in The Guide to the

Perplexed, the man who never makes a decision makes a decision.'

My mother frowned. 'What's that supposed to mean?'

Benny's hand was virtually swallowed by his beard as he scratched his chin. 'It means . . . Well . . . It means your decision is that you can't make a decision.'

Silence as the women struggled to absorb this – until my mother slapped the table and asked: 'So all right, clever Dick: what about God's decision? What about that, then? What made Him decide to persecute the Jews for thousands years? Why decide to have this rotten war?'

Benny Begel, sagely: 'Who's to know the intention of the Almighty? And if we did know – there'd be no free will, would there?'

My mother's eyes narrowed. 'Free veal? Why free veal? Where free veal? What's the catch?'

'Not veal, missus. It's mine double-yous.' He took a deep breath. 'Free *will*.' (Despite the effort, it still came out as veal.) 'What means to say the choice. Like it says in The Tree Of Life, you always got to have the choice from good and evil. If not, we'd already be in Heaven. And if we was, Heaven'd be no reward. You follow? So the choice of good must mean to sacrifice and suffer. Otherwise the wicked – well, they'd also go to Heaven.'

My mother opened her mouth, but before she could speak Mrs Block asked: 'What about them wealthy Jews? Like the Rothschilds and Waley-Cohens and Montagus and them Sassoons? How they supposed to suffer when they're rolling in it?'

A knowing 'Ah-ha!' from my mother. 'So that's what's worrying you.' As the others looked at her questioningly, she gave a shrug of contempt for their obtuseness. 'Butchers,' she explained, as though to retarded four-year-olds. After further stares: 'It stands to reason, no? Maybe they aren't Rothschilds, but they're not short of a thousand or two. It's logic. That's the worry, eh Mrs Block?'

The butcher's widow threw up her hands. 'I've said a million-and-one times: Hymie was just a hand from Solly Kugel.'

'And I've said a million-and-two times, some hands can hold a fortune,' my mother retorted. She held out her own. 'With mine arthritis – another of God's decisions! – I couldn't hold tuppence. But butchers? They got hands like frying pans. So don't talk to me about hands.'

'You and your butchers make me sick,' said Mrs Block tiredly. 'You got nothing better to talk about?' She turned to Benny Begel. 'Here

I am supposed to have more millions than Rothschild, but you know something? To talk about finding me a husband is such rubbish I wouldn't have for a new corset for the wedding. So to think of a dowry yet?'

'These days dowries aren't so important,' said Benny Begel soothingly. 'There's men with money who don't ask from even a farthing. Just the wife.'

'Them that marry for money usually earn it,' said Mrs Klopps wisely.

Mrs Krenk: 'If you're so good at finding husbands, what about finding mine?'

Benny clicked his teeth. 'He still hasn't turned up? A shame. Really, missus, a crying shame. But finding? Me, I don't go in for that sort of trade. You need more like the police.'

'The police!' My mother's shoulders shrugged upwards to her ears. 'What do they know? If you ask me, they're all in it together. Like when Mrs Myers from Chicksand Street lost her teeth in the blackout and asked the police to find. They said they had more important things. But what's more important than the teeth, eh girls? Without them you don't eat. And if you don't eat you starve to death. So if not wanting to find her teeth don't mean they want to starve her to death, what does it mean?'

'Teeth is useful,' Mrs Krenk agreed.

'Don't start again with the usefuls,' said my mother hotly. 'Though it does remind me. Talking of the police also reminds me: we got to remember to report that Rosie Speck.'

'A nice girl,' said Benny Begel. 'Now looking after the cousin in Hackney.'

My mother snorted. 'She taken you in too, eh? You also fallen for that cock-and-bull story?'

Benny finger-curled his beard. 'Story? How come story?'

My mother threw up her hands. 'You mean you don't know about the sewing-up of the bowels?'

Benny considered this. 'The bowels.' He pulled at his nose. 'Rabbi Berman, the Sage of Kandover, said—' He was interrupted by the arrival of Uncle Ben who demanded to see everyone's Identity Card.

'What's this new madness?' my mother howled.

Uncle Ben stared at her with as much graveness as he could manage. 'Who are you?'

'Who . . . Who . . .' My mother swallowed. 'Who . . . Am . . . I?' With a shriek: 'You gone even more *meschugger* – more potty?'

As she picked up a fork and made as though to stab him in the throat with it, Ben said hurriedly: 'All right, I'll take your word for it.

Just this once.' To Benny Begel: 'But what about you?'

'Well, what about me?'

'Where's your Identity Card? How do I know you're not one of them Fifth Columns? A spy?'

My mother screamed: 'Spy? You mean like with the armpits? *Oi gevult!*'

'Ben, you're up to your jokes again,' said Mrs Krenk kindly.

'It's no joke,' Ben assured her.

'And you're no joke neither,' said Benny Begel hotly. To my mother: 'I don't know nothing from armpits, but you hear what he got up to with the brush and paint the other day?'

'What now, Ben?' my mother asked wearily.

'The Government. They painted out the signposts,' her brother explained. 'So if the Germans come they won't know where they are. Not only in the country they painted, but here in London.'

'Sure I know it,' my mother replied. 'Previous Zanzibar Terrace was in the Borough Stepney. Now they painted out the Stepney, so God alone knows where we are. But what's with you also painting?'

'Suppose them Germans (may they be spared old age) do come – like from up the river, which is what you're always saying. So all right, they don't know if they're in the West End, East End or the other end. But they see the shops. And even if they don't speak English, they know what the Shield from David is, eh? They know the shops is Kosher, which also means Jewish. And who will they pick on if not the Yiddisher people? So I painted out all the Shields from David.'

My mother shook her head. '*Aie, aie aie* . . . So now it's not enough I don't know whether I'm in Stepney or Timbuctoo, thanks to you I don't know who's Kosher or not.'

'Much good such painting-out will do,' said Mrs Klopps sourly. 'You mean that with names like Levy and Cohen and Goldberg and Isaacs and what have you on the shops, the Germans won't know they're Jewish? With or without Stars of David?'

'You're right, missus,' said Ben excitedly. 'Tonight I'll go round and also paint out the names.'

'Haven't you done enough for the war already?' my mother pleaded. 'Shouldn't you let someone else have a turn?'

'Can't do enough,' said Ben, frowning. 'Like if they do come it isn't easy for women to know about the left breast, right breast, throat and belly . . . With the bayonet,' he explained to my mother's stupefied friends. 'So I heard about them Gurkhas also being in the war. Like they was in the last one, which made me remember they got what they call the kukris to kill with. Easier for the women to use. I'll make. And you ladies'll be the first to get. I swear.'

My mother, elbows on table, held her head in her hands and stared at him. 'Cookery? All of a sudden you're going to do the cookery? Over my dead body! So all right, I agree: women are better at the cookery. And if it comes to cooking killing the lousy Germans, certain people could be made generals and given medals by the King from England.' Voice rising: 'But what's this madness of you doing it first and then giving to us? You mean you'll test on us to see if it kills, you madman?'

'And what's with gherkins?' asked Mrs Krenk. 'I know they give the wind, but where you going to find gherkins these days?'

My mother: 'That's true. And what's also true is not only the gherkins: if you want to kill with rotten cooking, where you going to get the rations?'

There was a clatter on the stairs as Uncle Mendel came down with Aunt Zillah. 'I heard voices,' said my uncle, 'and came down to see who was here. I—' He broke off as my mother stood and saluted. 'W-what's this?'

'Go light the gas on the cooker,' my mother

replied with a giggle. 'Your wife's going to win the war for us.'

My mother's cronies went, but Uncle Mendel urged Benny to stay for a while to discuss the progress of the war. 'I'll tell you how I see what they call the situation,' he began portentously as he poured tea now diluted to pale yellow translucence – then went on to dismiss the Blitz, the Italian invasion of Greece, and the British successes in the Western Desert in a sentence. 'What's really important,' he whispered, 'is the shortage underwear.

'I was at the pictures earlier on – the one at the Troxy with Charlie Laughton as a paintist with some potty name like Rememberance or something. A load of rubbish. I like pictures that are more from real life. Like the other one that was showing, with Whatsit . . .' A gesture of impatience. 'You know, the one that looks like the one with the moustache who had the aggravations with the taxi cabs in Chicago with Alice Faye. He also invented the telephone.

'No matter. 'Cause in this picture there weren't no telephones. Only salmon. For there he was – and may God in Heaven strike me dead and then give me back my foreskin if I lie – there he was growing tin salmon on his own doorstep. 'Cause he also had the factory –

which was why he had the trouble with the brother over the girl who stuck the labels on the tins. So anyway, it goes to show, huh?'

'What goes to show what?' asked a puzzled Benny Begel as he pushed a hand under his cap and scratched his head. 'You're harder to follow than Cabbala.'

'It goes to show,' said Uncle Mendel tetchily, 'that in America there's opportunity. Like with the tin salmon. Here you can't find (except on the Black Market, which I won't touch with a bargepole). Over there they grow. You follow? . . . *Aaach!* what's the good talking? The answer is to go yourself. And I will, once this lousy war's over and I got the capital. So all I want from you is to find wallpaper.'

'Wallpaper?' Benny echoed weakly.

'Sure wallpaper,' said Mendel firmly.

'Look, mister,' said Benny, voice quavery, 'I know I'm a simpleton. A dummy. No good but to carry sacks of begels and do a bit for ARP. We know that. So to talk of shortage underwear, then some picture with tinned salmon, and then from the wallpaper . . .' He threw up his hands. 'It's too much for an ignoramus.'

'Sure it is,' Mendel agreed. His chest swelled and he flicked at his moustache spikes. 'After all, like you say, you fetch and carry the begels, while me – I'm the businessman. The dealer. What's more, you wasn't at the Troxy today. What I'm getting at . . .' He broke off and looked cunningly at Benny Begel. 'Never mind what I'm getting at . . . Top Secret . . . You follow? Let's leave it like this: you go round the East End, right? You meet people. So if you know where I can get hold of wallpaper just let me know.' Another inflation of chest then, grandly: 'I'll make you what they call an agent. *My* agent. On commission. Just tell me where there's wallpaper and I'll see you all right. Can I say fairer?'

As Benny Begel left the cellar he turned, his beard an agitated twitch. 'This . . . this wallpaper . . . Well I mean . . . Colour. Pattern. Quality.'

Mendel shrugged. 'Colour, *shmuller*. Pattern, *shmattern*. Quality, *shmol* . . .' He stopped and frowned. 'Quality. Sure quality. Of course quality. So OK, the colour and pattern don't matter, but if you can get thick, get.'

Benny stumbled up the stairs. When she heard the front door slam, my mother plucked at her brother's sleeve. 'Mendel dolly, I don't want to question. I mean, you're the genus, and I saw you in black and white doing the eyeballs with Benny Begel like a real businessman. A dealer. But . . .' An apologetic smile. 'I got to admit I also don't follow. I mean to say . . . So there's a shortage underwear. That I understand. Then there's Charlie Whoever and the tinned salmon – and now suddenly there's thick wallpaper. I'm at sixes and sevens.'

Mendel winked and wagged a finger. Tucking his thumbs into the armholes of his waistcoat: 'I didn't want to give the game away to Benny. That's where being a businessman comes in. That's why mum's the word. You got to make what they call a snap decision.' He clicked his fingers to demonstrate. 'And it come to me in the pictures.'

'With this Charlie and the tinned salmon?'

An exasperated growl. 'Between the pictures there's the newsreel and the organist, no? And also . . .' voice rising with excitement '. . . a picture from the Ministry. Only five minutes long, but like a real picture. About the shortage underwear. And this man very high up in the Government showed that brown paper keeps you just as warm. But I'm no fool. They can't bamboozle Mendel Abrams. For don't I know that brown paper is just as short as underwear? So what's the answer?' He looked around him, but before any of us could venture a guess: 'It came to me in a blink of the eyeballs. So sure I should live to see the Statue Liberty – a blink. For that's what makes a typhoon different from the rest, like with Spencer Tracy when he bought Texas: the snap decision.

'So quick as a blink, I thought of white paper, greaseproof paper, tissue paper. But they're also in short supply.' Triumphantly: 'So why not wallpaper? Eh? Huh? What about that? Because all over there must be a million rolls wallpaper nobody wants. Think for yourself: who wants to paper walls these days? Is it logic? To paper walls for the *vershtinkener* Germans to bomb to pieces? Does it stand to reason? So with mine agent, Benny Begel, I'll strike while the Aaron is hot as the saying goes. I'll buy up the wallpaper, cut into yard lengths and make a fortune. A fortune!' he roared.

Voice dropping: 'But I wasn't going to give the game away to Benny, was I? Let him think what he likes. Let him wonder.' Voice rising again: 'When he's still *shlepping* begels we'll be in America with fitted carpets, a doorbell and telephone, and inside lav and bathroom, darkies dancing in their white ties and tails, change our shirts twice a week, and a motor car half the length of Zanzibar Terrace with a driver in a peaked hat and them gaiters.'

'Like they say in Yiddish,' Granny Abrams began, but Mendel interrupted with: 'I don't want to know what they say in Yiddish.'

Granny Abrams nodded. 'I know the Jews

born here don't like to talk Yiddish,' she said thoughtfully in Yiddish. 'When they hear it they're ashamed. But what else can the old people talk? In the Old Country we wasn't even allowed to learn from Polish. So Yiddish. All right, I got a few words English, but without the Yiddish I'd be dumb. Is that what you want?' Mendel opened his mouth to protest, but my grandmother held up a hand. 'From hundreds years people have talked Yiddish. Even my prayer books are in Yiddish. Now people are ashamed.' She sighed. 'And there's also what your poor father used to say. Remember? That Yiddish is not only the language of the Jews, it's the history of the Jews – thousands of years of tears put into words.'

Mendel again opened his mouth, but my mother said quickly: 'From this wallpaper you're going to make enough money for all them things – the motor car (a motor car yet!) and the fitted carpets and what have yous?'

'It's a start,' said Mendel wearily. 'How many times do I have to tell you 'til I'm blue in the face that everyone has to start somewhere? Look at f'rinstance Monty Burton. Didn't he have to start with one lousy suit? Eh? And look at him now – thousands of shops selling suits by the million. And from what? One stinking rotten two-piece. So you wait and see:

from that wallpaper we'll end up knee-deep in all the underwear you want.'

'You know what we done in Poland in the winter?' asked Granny Abrams. When Mendel shook his head she said: 'We shivered,' and laughed so much her upper dentures fell into her lap.

NINE

The winter of 1940/1941 was indeed severe, but my uncle made no fortune from wallpaper vests: the material proved to be virtually unobtainable. Mendel refused to accept this as another manifestation of the austerity of the times: to his dying day he held Benny Begel responsible, convinced that his agent had betrayed him by cornering all available wallpaper for himself. '*Oi*, what a ruffian! Naturally the *dumkopf* don't know what it's for. What to do with. Why he wants. But he hears a businessman, a dealer, is after it, so he buys. Just for the sake of having. So I can't get, and that *schmock's* got millions rolls going to waste. I . . . I could get him twenty years' hard labour for hoarding.'

‘Quite right,’ my mother agreed. ‘It’s not nice doing you down like that. Ben was right with the Identification Cards.’ When Mendel raised questioning eyebrows: ‘Whose side he on if not the Germans (may their doctors grow rich), letting people freeze to death because they’re short of your wallpaper. You’re right – go get him arrested. Or you want I should? It won’t take a minute to put on my hat and coat.’

‘Sit. Sit,’ said Mendel hurriedly. ‘But in America I’d give a nod and a wink to that fellow with the Italianer name, and before you could say knife that Benny would be put on what they call the spot. Like James Cagney – which was before he went screaming to the ’lectric chair – done with Georgie Raft and the other one. Dead they was.’

‘You got to be careful with electric,’ my mother agreed. ‘And also the spots. Can be catching.’

Mendel flapped a hand. ‘Don’t worry from spots. Don’t worry from Benny (may the worms in his belly get St Vitus dance). I got another deal going. You remember with the elastic in the last war?’

‘Remember?’ my mother breathed. ‘Can I forget?’

‘So this time I got elastic waistbands for trousers. By the gross. Because it stands to reason, no? Whatever else goes short, people still got to wear trousers. And isn't there a shortage buttons? So without buttons you can't wear the braces. And leather for the belts is also very short. So how to keep up the trousers if not with elastic waistbands? The poor can use string, but up West? You take my word, Minnie – so sure I should live to see grandchildren there'll be people queuing knee-deep in the street for Mendel Abrams's elastic waistbands. Even Monty Burton personal. May God—' He was interrupted by the Alert. With a sigh and much shaking of his head he went to help his mother down to the cellar.

Since the absurd had become the norm in so many areas of life, nights in the cellar were now as natural as nights in bedrooms had been. We'd settle down as best we could: Granny Abrams on the sofa, my mother and Aunt Zillah in armchairs, Uncle Mendel on the table, whoever else was at home mastering the technique of sleeping in a stiff-backed kitchen chair. When we were away from home during the day, sirens sent us to the nearest shelter, although there were exceptions: my mother refusing to allow 'them dirty rotten Germans' make her lose her place in the queue when there was hake or halibut to be had (even though the fishmonger temporarily shut up shop); Mendel determined to discover what happened at the end of *Target For Tonight*, *Fifth Avenue Girl*, *Maytime*, or some equally vital film.

The Blitz ended at Whitsun, but since we realized this only in hindsight, the family spent their nights in the shelter until VE-day.

Bombing, shortages, the deaths of loved ones and friends, the mixed fortunes of the Allies – all were accepted fairly philosophically by the family. Motivating this were the optimistic fatalism and patriotism shared with the rest of the population, but Jewishness added an extra dimension to the certitude of final victory: the unshakable faith, seldom voiced, but deep in the collective subconscious, in God's promise of survival. Not survival of the individual, but of the Jews as a people, for despite centuries of Hitlers, there still had to be Jews for Messiah, at the end of days, to lead to the Promised Land. And that survival, historically, was earned by sacrifice and suffering.

The list of items in short supply grew daily – from needles, cotton, brooms, alcohol and flypapers to lawnmowers, alarm clocks, hats and cosmetics. The catalogue seemed endless, but my mother shrugged off most of it.

'Crockery we got. Maybe some's chipped and cracked, but we got. Knives and forks we got. Furniture?' She laughed. 'Linen we got. Sweets?' A grudging admission that she was fond of a bit of fudge and a sugared almond. 'As for toothbrushes, you do what I used to do: a bit of soap on the finger and rub.'

'And from between the teeth a hairpin,' said Granny Abrams who, having just finished her dinner, was able to demonstrate with her dentures.

My mother reserved her rage for what really mattered: the shortage of food. 'So all right, rationing is rationing,' she conceded. 'I heard on the wireless only the other day that it's fair. Everyone gets a share. So we won't talk about that. But what about the things that aren't rationed, eh? Answer me that. Personal, I put it down to the lousy Government being dirty anti-semitics.'

Mendel frowned at her. 'How come?'

'How come? I'll tell you how come. Because how come all the things Yiddisher people eat aren't on the rationing, but you can't get? That's how come. I'll give a f'rinstance. Smoked salmon, which you know full well is Jewish. When was there a proper Jewish engagement or wedding or *bar mitzvah* or funeral' (she spat three times to ward off the evil eye) 'without smoked salmon? But when you seen smoked salmon lately? Answer me that. And from where does it come? From the Scottish.' She looked triumphantly round the table. 'So I'm ignorant, never went to school proper, but that I know, huh? Scottish. And the Scottish is now working for Hitler all of a sudden? They can't send by the train no more?

'And another thing: chopped liver. Also Jewish. So what's in chopped liver? If you don't know by now I'll tell you. There's chicken livers. Which stands to reason. Not rationed, but when did Hymie Black – or any other butcher come to that – have chicken livers? Also you need chicken fat. Likewise, when did you last see a decent tray chicken fat in the shops? . . . And you also need onions. Onions!' A *pshaw* of anger. 'No one's never seen an onion for years . . . Eggs also you need. But chickens don't lay 'em no more. Ach, it makes me sick.

'And there's lemon tea: also Jewish. But I've forgotten what a lemon looks like. Instead they give us them flavoured crystals . . . And what about *kasha*?' With another triumphant smirk: 'What in English they call the Canadian buckwheat.' A smug: 'That I also know . . . Them Canadas also working for Hitler? (may he go bankrupt). I thought they was over here helping us. Mendel, you got to get their armpits given a thorough examination.'

Mendel groaned. 'I curse the day I ever mentioned armpits.'

'Another thing: carp for *gefilte* fish. And the most important of the lot – *lockshen* soup. For the blood, the heart, the health and strength. And which also needs eggs, chickens—'

Uncle Ben interrupted with: 'Feed.'

My mother glared at him. 'What does that mean?'

'Them chickens you're on about.'

'So what about them?'

'There's a shortage feed.'

'Sure there's a shortage. We don't get fed.' She clicked her teeth at her brother's thick-headedness.

'No, Minnie, I mean feed for the chickens. The . . . well, whatever it is they feed them on.'

My mother frowned as she considered this. Then, with a cry that caused us all to jump: 'So that's the answer!'

'What is?' asked Aunt Zillah.

'Look,' said my mother patiently, 'the food special to Yiddisher people isn't on the ration. But you can't get. Ben says because of the feed. So ration this feed. Then the chickens and the carp and the smoked salmon and whatever'll get the rations, and when they've had their rations we'll get ours. Special for the Jews. Like now we don't take the bacon and ham and pork and rabbits and what have yous, so we'll get Jewish food instead.

'Let the food they haven't got be put on the ration and we'll get. Just so long they don't make the ration too small.

'I'll get Mrs Krenk write a postcard. In the meantime, Mendel, first thing in the morning you got to go see the Town Hall. Put your foot down. Tell them, eyeball to eyeball, that this war won't last for ever, and we Yiddisher people won't forget in a hurry how they're doing us out of our rations.'

'I – I got very important business tomorrow,' said Mendel. Conspiratorially: 'A buyer for the elastic waistbands.' He rubbed his hands and hummed a few bars of 'Yankee Doodle Dandy'.

'So I'll go myself,' said my mother resignedly. 'I haven't got enough to do with the shopping and cooking, but I'll go.'

And she did – putting on her best hat and dragging me with her 'as a witness' to Stepney Town Hall, my protests at being absent from work dismissed with: 'Say you've been blown to pieces. These days it happens all the time.'

The aged and mournful man at the door, hands deep in his overcoat pockets, cigarette glued to his lower lip, greeted us with: 'Close the door, mate. It's freezing in here.'

'Course you're freezing,' my mother agreed. 'You don't eat proper.'

'Eat proper? Who does these days?'

'Just like I was saying,' my mother approved. 'So take us to the Mayor.'

'What?'

'You got cloth ears all of a sudden? The Mayor. The Mayor from Stepney.'

'You got a 'pointment?'

My mother patted his arm. At her most ingratiating: 'Just say it's Mrs Ashe. A poor widow with arthritis. From Zanzibar Terrace, former Daffodil Square. I once had dealings with his partner in Kilburn about the trenches. Just say. Tell him it's about the chickens with no livers. He'll know.'

The doorman: 'Is – is it about the rations then?'

My mother: 'Naturally the rations. Of course the rations. What else if not the rations?'

The doorman wriggled a mauve sponge of a nose. 'Ah, rations . . . Now if you was pregnant . . .' but got no further as my mother raised her umbrella in a manner that made it no less formidable than any of Uncle Ben's bayonets.

'Are you 'sinuating?'

The doorman backed to the wall with a panicky: 'Me, 'sinuating? I haven't 'sinuated since Gawd alone knows. Me prostate. That and being seventy-four. All I'm saying is that for extra rations, for a Green Ration Book, you got to be pregnant.'

'You filthy swine!' my mother screamed. 'You mean to get a bit of chopped liver I got . . . got . . .' As words failed her she tightened her grip on the umbrella and thrust it to within an inch of the doorman's larynx. 'Left breast, right breast and guts, you dog's-body!' she howled.

Desperately he waved an arm. 'Try in there, mate,' he managed, pointing to an open door.

'So why not say in the first place instead of trying to bamboozle me with filthy talk, you . . . you armpit!' my mother cried, and swept through the door. As I followed her I saw that on the door's glass panel were painted the words: CEMETERY INQUIRIES.

A ruddy-faced man in his fifties looked up from a copy of *Film Fun*. A nasal: 'Yes, darlin'?'

My mother's passion evaporated as she took in his well-starched white collar and tightly knotted black tie, and the enamelled shields in the lapels of his blue serge jacket carrying the council coat of arms. She almost curtsied. Shyly: 'It's about the feed for the Kosher food, mister. Like the chicken livers. To say nothing of the smoked salmon, the lemon tea or the *kasha*. You got to do something. After all, you're in a position. So be a *mensch* – a man – and act. Show what you're made of. Don't let them twist you round their little finger. So what about it, eh? *Please?* To help a poor widow with no husband to speak up for her.'

The man gaped and ran a finger round the inside of his collar. 'What you on about, darlin'? . . . 'Ang on a minute, though . . . In all that rigmarole, wasn't there something about chicken livers?'

'Of course there was something about chicken livers. But that's only the start. There's—'

'And you got a complaint about them, darlin'?'

'Complaint?' A short, mirthless laugh. 'It's more like the medical d'rectory.'

'Yes . . . well, darlin', in that case it's either the 'Ealth or the Food.'

My mother chewed at her lower lip and shook her head from side to side. 'Food sounds more like. Health we already got. It may be bad, but we got. Food we haven't got. So what you going to do?'

'Me, darlin'? What am I to do? I'm not the 'Ealth and I'm not the Food am I? So I can't 'elp, unless . . . well, has someone died?' He tugged at an ear lobe. 'Except even then, what with you being of the Jewish persuasion (which I take it you are, darlin') I still can't 'elp. You go to the synagogue when people die, don't you?'

My mother paled. 'Jew-Jewish? Synagogue? D-died? You mean we got to die before we get extra Kosher food? What new anti-semitic filth is this? *Aie, aie, aie* . . . And another thing: what's with persuasion? You think I had to be persuaded to be Jewish?' She flapped a hand. 'For such a blessing I didn't need no persuading. It was one of God's chosen bargains.'

'You got to go to the proper department, darlin',' said the man desperately.

My mother gripped her umbrella, but managed a sympathetic: 'I follow you, mister. I saw in the *Sunday Pictorial*: what they call the tape. Nowadays everything they wrap up in it. Everything.'

'Tape,' the man echoed.

'Sure tape,' said my mother vehemently. 'My brother the businessman tried to get. A man in your position must've heard.'

Silence until I remembered Uncle Mendel's abortive search. 'Red tape, Mum?'

'Of course red. I saw in black and white. So who's the man I see about the shortage feed for the food?'

Eyeing his comic, and plainly anxious to

return to it: 'Feed . . . for the food.'

'I said. Feed for the food. Whatever chickens and smoked salmon eat these days.'

He licked his lips. 'I think you need the Ministry of Agriculture and Fisheries, darlin'. Whitehall.'

'Whitehall?' A long exhalation. 'You mean from the King? The Government?'

'Something like that.'

'*Oi veh!*' She wriggled her shoulders. 'The Government yet! Winston Churchill. Eden . . .' She gasped. 'Eden! Of course Eden! The Jewish one. Former Yidden from the Garden Eden . . . Naturally Eden. The religious one who always wears a hat. He'll know. Understand.'

'But . . . but he's the Foreign Secretary, darlin'.'

My mother spread her hands. 'The Jews wasn't original foreign? . . . So I'll go see him . . .' As she realized the enormity of such an undertaking: 'Well, maybe not personal, what with the arthritis and bunions and cooking and other aggravations, but I got brothers. One very high-up in the ARP, the other an important businessman. Also a daughter very big in the Red Cross. And when they say they represent me – me, Minnie Ashe, who was told personal by the Mayor Stepney . . . Well, it stands to reason, no?'

The man's eyes bulged, but before he could speak I moved behind my mother, pursed my lips, frowned, nodded, winked, gesticulated – anything I could think of short of words to convey the need to humour her. He got the message, rose to his feet and clasped his hands behind his back. 'Well, darlin', I've a lot to do. You know how it is, bein' mayor. Open things, shut things, hand out a few medals here and there, visit the bomb sites, go to the hospital . . .' He strolled up and down the tiny office then paused at the window. The sight of the Tower of London provided an added: 'Pop over to see the Crown Jewels are OK . . . You must understand, darlin'.'

'Sure I understand . . . *Aie*, the Crown Jewels yet! . . . You're a real gentleman to spare me the time, mister.' My mother searched her carrier bag, produced a newspaper-wrapped package and took from it two sandwiches. 'It's dangerous to do all that opening and closing the Crown Jewels on an empty stomach. So take. Eat. Enjoy. It's not salt beef, which is marvellous for the opening, but shoulder lamb. If you don't like fat (but what can I do when that Hymie Black – who you should also keep an eye on – says it's all he's got?) so rub on the chest. Wonderful for the consumption.'

'B-but—'

'No buts,' said my mother firmly, placing

the sandwiches on the desk. 'Don't worry about me, although it's nice of you to take an interest. So eat hearty and thank you very much. Simey, say thank you to the gentleman.'

I said thank you and hid the lettering on the door with my body as my mother almost bowed her way out. In the entrance hall the man in the overcoat squawked and hurried down a corridor. My mother gave his back a withering glare, a wave of her umbrella and a contemptuous 'Dog's-body.'

In the street she beamed at me. 'A nice fellow eh, that mayor? A proper *mensch.*' She whistled. 'To see the Mayor, yet! Personal! Me, Minnie Ashe. It's given me palpitations. I've gone hot and cold all over. But it goes to show what you can do when you try . . . 'Though I must say he gave me a funny turn with that mad talk about persuaded Jews having to die to get more rations.' She shivered. Quickly recovering, a generous: 'Everyone's got their funny ways.'

Another long whistle, followed by a giggle. 'Wait 'til the others hear. One in the eye for them, eh? Huh? Green with envy they'll be. Never believe—'cept you was there in black and white as a witness.'

There was indeed collective disbelief that evening when my mother told the family that she'd been to the Town Hall to give the Mayor a good talking to – until I assured them that I'd been with her. Incredulity turned to awesome respect – except for a sour and sulky Uncle Mendel.

'The Mayor,' he sneered. 'So what's a mayor? Mayor, *schmayor*. Wouldn't I've gone to see him if I didn't have business on? Mayors! What's so marvellous going to see a mayor? Like God or something in the burning bush? What is he in real life, anyway? I got on good authority he's actually a draper, like the one previous.'

'Selfridge's was a draper,' said Aunt Zillah. 'Army and Navy and Marks and Spencer and Peter and Robinson was also a draper. I only wish I had their money.'

'Gardner up the road was a draper,' said Uncle Ben, 'and he got Gardner's Corner named after him. Go down in history like Vimy Ridge and Aldgate Pump.'

'We was drapers,' said Granny Abrams. 'Why be ashamed of drapers if your own father (may he rest in peace) was one? Between being in the wet fish and the second-hand pianos, we also had a drapery shop. In Bethnal Green Road . . . Your father saw Katan with the limp was doing good in the drapery, so he also opened.' She smiled. 'And also went bust. It just proves: you can't chew with somebody else's teeth.'

'What does that mean?' asked Mendel.

'It means you got to stick to what you know.'

'Don't eat your heart out,' said my mother soothingly. 'Forget such things. Think of the future.'

My grandmother shook her head. 'Forget? Like they say in Yiddish, if we could forget we'd never mourn. And as for the future, like the Ritziner Rabbi used to say: today is your future, because tomorrow may not come . . . So what was I saying? . . . Ah, yes . . . Don't be so quick to make fun of the drapers, Mendel.'

'Not drapers?' Mendel cried angrily. 'Mayors! What I'm saying is mayors. F'rinstance, in America people like Edward Arnold buy ten a penny.'

'So go buy,' my mother urged. 'At that price you'd do yourself a favour.'

As Uncle Mendel ground his teeth, Ben said: 'You done a good job, Minnie. But you haven't said why you went to the Town Hall. And what happens now.'

My mother gave a self-deprecating shrug. 'Well, to tell the truth it's up to Mendel.'

A suspicious: 'How me?'

My mother stroked his sleeve. 'You're the genus, no? The businessman. The one sold the elastic waistbands.'

Mendel's moustache-ends seemed to self-stiffen with pride. 'So?'

'So for you mayors don't mean from nothing. But . . . Well . . . the Whitehall does mean, no? Eh? The Gov'ment. The King from England personal. Surely that must mean?'

'Of course it means.'

'So like I said, you're the genus. The head from the family. The one to make decisions. Snap the fingers.'

'What else if not the head?' Mendel demanded, this time twirling the spikes of his moustache. 'What else if not the decisions?'

'So you're the one to go see Anthony Eden.' Ignoring the stares, she went on to explain the feed, the Ministry of Agriculture, the Foreign Secretary, and how the Mayor of Stepney said his name could be used by way of introduction. 'I'd go myself,' she concluded, 'but you just said you're the head of the family. The genus. The businessman. The one to make with the eyeballs. The one who can make them sit up. So you go to Whitehall . . . All you got to do is mention Minnie Ashe and the Mayor. Like I read in the paper: Downing Street. Number Ten. He might even offer you a position.'

'Now that could be good for the Jews for a change,' said Granny Abrams.

'Of course if he goes it could be good,' said

my mother. 'Didn't I always say they needed a Yiddisher brain like him in the Government?'

'I mean the number ten,' my grandmother explained in Yiddish. 'Always been a lucky number. Like it says in the Duties of the Heart: there's the Ten Commandments, the ten plagues on the Egyptians, the ten days of penitence, the ten generations from Adam to Noah, the Ten Tribes . . . And the most important: it takes ten to make a quorum in the synagogue . . . There's others, but I forget. So go see this number ten Minnie's on about . . . In any case, what harm can it do?'

Uncle Mendel tugged at his waistcoat and straightened his tie. 'Sure I'll go. Of course I'll go. And when they know Mendel Abrams is coming it'll be like Edward G when he took over the barber shop. They'll jump all right.'

'Put on your good suit,' said Aunt Zillah. 'Show that we might ask a favour, but we're not beggars.'

'When you going?' asked Ben.

An airy: 'Maybe one day next week.'

'Why not tomorrow?' his wife demanded.

'Why not tomorrow? . . . Because . . .' A defiant: 'Well, because I say so.' A conciliatory: 'The best suit needs a press.'

'I'll do tonight.'

'I also got other business!' Mendel roared. 'The money from them waistbands got to be invested. Strike while the Aaron. You follow? Like when Tim Holt sold the gold to the Ringo Kid. And I also got to make the 'rangements. What they call in America the . . .' Abandoning his search for the word: 'The whatsits . . . When Edward Arnold and Georgie Brent went to see Raymond Whosit in what they call the White House, you think they just caught the 88 bus? Is it logic? Does it stand to reason? Course not. It took months of 'rangin with the lawyers and senators and the Secret Service.'

Aunt Zillah, glumly: 'By then we could starve to death.'

My mother: 'What's with senna? You saying this Eden suffers the constipation? (may it never happen here). If so, you tell him straight that if he does what you ask and we get the proper Jewish food, it'll be over in no time. Better than all the senna and Ex-Lax and syrup of figs put together, tell him. A good bowl *lockshen* soup every day and he'll go regular like clockwork. Just ask Ruthie if all them top doctors in the Red Cross don't agree with me.'

'Not senna!' Mendel thundered. 'I said—'

'I'm off Fire Watching,' Ben interrupted. He gave his mother a kiss and left the cellar.

Granny Abrams shook her head. 'What a *meschuggener*, to go out every night watching fires.'

‘Not watching them, Granny,’ I explained. ‘Watching *out* for them. In every street—’

I got no further as my mother pummelled the top of my head with her fists. ‘How dare you contradict your grandmother, you Cossack toerag?’ she howled. ‘Because I let him come with me to see the Mayor, he got ideas he knows better than his grandmother. You should have your mouth washed out with acid, you guttersnipe!’

‘Enough already!’ Granny Abrams commanded.

‘So give him right,’ said my mother bitterly as she exercised her fingers. ‘I’m crippled to death with arthritis and aggravations, yet for your sake I give him a hiding he won’t forget in a hurry – but you say stop. OK, I’ll stop. I’m in the wrong and he’s in the right, is that it?’

‘There isn’t enough fighting in the world already?’ asked my grandmother.

‘So that means this low-life Count Potocki of a swinehound can get away with blue murder?’

‘Minnie’s right,’ said Aunt Zillah. ‘You got to give ’em what for every so often, even if they haven’t done nothing you know about, because there must be plenty you don’t know about that they have actually done. You follow? It works out fair in the end. So this one . . .' She jerked a thumb at Mendel '. . . how do I know what he gets up to?'

'G-get up to?' her husband spluttered. 'Me?'

'How do I know you don't go gambling or . . . Well, why not other women?'

A mad gurgle of a laugh. 'W-women? Me? At my age? . . . Chance'd be a fine thing.'

'Dogs chase after cars,' said Aunt Zillah sagely. 'When they catch them they can't drive 'em. But does it stop them chasing?'

'What you're saying isn't nice, Zillah,' said my mother severely. 'I don't like such talk.'

'Take no notice,' said Mendel wearily. 'It's always been her nature. Like they say in Yiddish: if she'd been Eve she'd've counted Adam's ribs every night.'

A few days later Mendel arrived home with a carrier bag from which, after unwrapping a dozen protective newspapers, he produced a half-bottle of whisky.

'Where d'you get that?' Ben demanded. 'The Black Market? 'Cause if so I got to report you.'

'Black Market!' his brother roared. 'What you mean, Black Market? You know full well I never have dealings with them ruffians.'

'Then where you get it?'

'Lew Henry owed me a favour and sold me.'

'If he owed you a favour he should have given, not sold,' said Granny Abrams.

'These days it's a favour to be able to buy at the proper price,' Mendel assured her.

'He didn't have kummel? I like a drop of kummel for the digestion,' said his mother. 'No matter. We'll keep for something special.'

'Today's special,' said Mendel.

'Today?' Granny Abrams scratched her head. 'Memory's like teeth – the older you get the more you need, but the feebler they become. Because as you get older what else you got to do but eat and remember? So what is it? A birthday? Anniversary?'

'Elastic waistbands,' Mendel beamed.

Granny Abrams frowned. 'I thought you sold.'

A smug: 'Sure I sold. Thirty gross I sold. Morrie Gett who bought almost laughed up his sleeve when I told how much I wanted. Now he's laughing the other side of his face.'

'How come?' asked my mother.

'You haven't heard the news? That there's clothes rationing started?'

Aunt Zillah: 'Never!'

My mother shrugged. 'That's something they can ration 'til they're blue in the face. When was the last time anyone here bought clothes?'

'What you don't understand,' said Mendel,

'is there's going to be no more double-breasted, a limit on the number pockets and buttons, how wide is the turn-ups . . . And guess what? No elastic waistbands. May God strike me deaf, dumb and blind and then give me an affliction – no elastic waistbands. So I done a good deal huh?, and that Morrie Gett's eating his heart out and laughing the other side of his face.'

My mother whistled. 'Didn't I always say you was the genus? Didn't I always know? Now who can say different? If they do I'll report straight to the Town Hall . . . Which reminds me: when you going to see this Eden? Let me know in good time and I'll give soup to take instead of the senna.'

Mendel bared his teeth. Then a conspiratorial: 'Top Secret.'

My mother looked at him bleakly. 'Meaning?'

'Meaning I got other things to do!' Mendel screeched. A long exhalation of breath. 'Meaning I got to arrange. Fix. Like with Wassisname Beery – the one with the nose who was also on the Brooklyn Bridge and was in that foreign country in South America. To see the President there – *oi gevult*! – you'd never believe what he had to do to arrange. So if it takes time for him to fix with the President of South America, isn't it also going to take me time? Even if I am Mendel Abrams?'

'I know you're the genus like I said,' my mother ventured shyly, 'but you want I should have another word with the Mayor Stepney?'

'What's that . . . that rubbishy draper going to do? Apart from anything else, going to Whitehall can cost money.'

My mother clicked her teeth. 'You mean from the waistbands you didn't make enough profit for the bus fare?'

Uncle Mendel waved clenched fists above his head.'I mean that like with Wally Beery, you got to contribute to what they call the funds. Thousands it cost him to fix.'

An agonized '*Oi veh*' from my mother. Then a happy: 'Go Saturday.' To her perplexed brother an explanatory: 'Eden'll understand. Being the Sabbath he'll know you're not allowed to carry money. Say you'll post later . . . Even better, say it's the budget like with the shopping.'

'Elastic,' said Granny Abrams. Seeing us staring at her: 'Drapers got 'lastic, no? In the last war was the half-inch elastic. This time the waistbands. Elastic's been very good to us, so maybe Minnie's right: go see this mayor and ask what else from 'lastic you can buy.'

'I'm fed up to here . . .' Mendel demonstrated with a hand across his throat '. . . with mayors and drapers. Anyway, I got an investment for the waistband money.' He beamed at us. 'Tobacco. There's a shortage cigarettes, no? But like that Levinson you used to know in Kilburn, Minnie, there's this Mervyn Lee from Bow Road who also collected dog-ends in the streets for the unused tobacco. When he got blown up from that bomb that went off near the old Pavilion Jewish Theatre (may it never happen here) the widow was left with sacks of tobacco. Sacks of it. God alone knows what he was saving up for, but may the Almighty give me a black year if I lie – by the sackful.'

'Consumption you'll get by the sacckful,' said my mother.

'What does that mean?' her brother demanded.

'Cigarette ends it means. Who knows what filthy diseases these people who smoked them suffer from? And also from the pavements.' She shuddered. 'Coughing up the blood and the phlegm. Also the dogs.' She looked meaningfully at Mendel. 'And Diseases I Can't Even Mention.'

'You suppose I hadn't thought of that?' Mendel retorted. 'I'll fumigate.'

'Just don't bring in the house,' said his mother.

'I'll do in the yard,' her son promised her. 'I already got the sulphur candles.'

He did indeed disinfect the tobacco, and the result was a powdery abomination indistinguishable in taste and smell from pure sulphur. Sniffing at it as Uncle Mendel puffed cautiously at a Rizla-papered sample, my mother coughed, grimaced and managed: 'F-from this you're going to make a fortune?'

'Not . . . necessarily . . . a . . . fortune . . .' Mendel admitted between chokes. 'B-but a . . . a . . . start.' He ground the cigarette underfoot and cleared his lungs. 'Didn't Player himself have to start with one packet cigarettes? Likewise De Reszke and Woodbine and that other one. Didn't they have to make a start somewhere? So why not Mendel Abrams by selling in ounce packets?'

My mother, cautiously: 'Them others, they also started with dustbin powder?'

Mendel patted her head. 'These days people'll smoke anything.'

For once he was right.

My mother's account of her visit to the Mayor of Stepney was lavishly embroidered by time and telling, and for a while (to the ill-concealed annoyance of Uncle Mendel) she was something of a minor celebrity in the immediate neighbourhood of Zanzibar Terrace. But as she later admitted, it proved to be a mixed blessing.

On the one hand it was immensely gratifying to bully tradesmen with threats of reporting them to 'my friend the Mayor who knows Eden personal, and who'll get you hard labour for the way you're treating me, you dirty armpit'. On the other hand she was homed-in on by everyone with a complaint, from Mrs Krenk's demand that something should be done to find her mislaid husband, to dissatisfactions more endemic to the times – requests that she organize an efficient collection of domestic rubbish; improve the supply of wireless valves, hairpins, soft toilet paper and tin openers; get landlords to repair bomb-blasted shops and homes; arrange jobs in Reserved Occupations to avoid the call-up of loved ones . . .

She made evasive promises on the lines of 'I'll bring it up next time I see the Mayor Stepney,' then Solly Litvak's son, Mervyn, who'd been invalided out of the Army after losing an arm in the Western Desert, took a job with a firm of solicitors in the City. Mervyn was employed to run messages and keep the place tidy, but since he was the nearest thing to a free-of-charge legal expert in the area, my mother was spared further requests for assistance – to her obvious relief.

'It's not I don't want to help,' she rationalized, 'but it'd be wrong not to do Mervyn a turn, eh? After all, it's doing him a favour. Giving him practice. Helping him learn the trade.'

As for going to see Anthony Eden, the war was over before Uncle Mendel had time between business negotiations to complete the final arrangements.

Russia's entry into the war was greeted with mixed feelings.

'Apart from helping to win it's good for the workers,' my cousin Bernard assured us.

My mother: 'You mean we'll all get a five-pound note?'

My grandmother nodded. 'Good for the workers. But is it good for the Jews?'

'Aren't the Jews workers?' Bernard retorted.

Granny Abrams sighed. 'What I mean is like this . . . It was bad enough when they said the Polish Army was our friends. For in Poland who done the pogroms and killed the Yiddisher people if not the Polish Army? And they're our friends all of a sudden? I should invite for a glass lemon tea? My worst enemies should have such friends . . . Now it's the Russians. So who told the Poles and also his own Cossacks to start the pogroms if not the Tsar Russia?' She flapped a hand. 'Let the Germans and Poles and Russians kill each other 'til they're blue in the face.' Bitterly: 'When they're all dead and buried then maybe it'll be good for the Jews. Otherwise?' A dismissive shrug.

'But they killed the Tsar of Russia at the time of the Revolution,' cried an exasperated Bernard. 'Today half the Soviet government are Jews.'

'There's Jews and Jews,' said my mother knowingly. 'Like Kosher butchers is also supposed to be Jews.'

Uncle Ben: 'Them Russians was our allies in the last war.'

'Things do change,' Uncle Mendel assured his mother. 'Wasn't them Frenchies once our enemy? Like when they cut off Ronald Coleman's head . . . Even the Americans. May God strike me down dead and bury me alive if I lie – the Americans!' He looked at us in turn as though challenging denial. 'The Americans was our enemy! Didn't I see with my own eyeballs at the Troxy that they also had a revolution against us? Except they called it the War 'Dependence. With the Rebs and the Unions.'

'I read in the paper only the other day in black and white about the unions,' my mother agreed. 'They're always causing trouble. Here we are at war, and if that wasn't aggravation enough, the miners are on strike.' A thoughtful pause, then a triumphant: '*Ah-ha!* And didn't it say them Communists was behind it? So how come they're on our side? Working for the rotten Germans is more like.'

'Not trade unions!' Mendel bellowed. 'I'm on about . . .' His shoulders sagged. 'No matter. Forget it.'

'Uncle Mendel,' I ventured, 'aren't you mixing up the War of Independence with the American Civil War?'

'How dare you contradict your uncle!' my mother screamed as she gave me a mighty slap across the face. 'Here's Mendel, the genus who goes to the pictures regular like clockwork, and you . . . you snotty-nosed toerag . . .' After a pause for breath: 'Who are you to argue? To question? You should go on your bended knees and beg forgiveness. You should—'

'I did go to school,' I muttered as I edged out of range.

'So now he interrupts. Isn't it marvellous?' A mirthless cough of a laugh. 'I taught him to talk, and now he's trying to teach me to shut up.'

'I'm sorry!' I shouted as she advanced on me.

Sitting back again in her chair: 'Sorry? You're always sorry. Like your poor father used to say, if you didn't sin so much you wouldn't have to repent so much.'

'You got to understand,' said Bernard earnestly, 'that all politics are relative. Like . . . um . . . like Einstein. Relativity,' he added uncertainly.

'Einstein?' Uncle Mendel frowned. 'We got a relative called Einstein? Since when? And on whose side the family? Your father? If so it's news to me.'

Granny Abrams: 'There used to be an Einstein in Lodz when we was there. Not a relation, thank God. A moneylender. So he got driven out by the Chief Rabbi there who told him he wasn't a Jew no more, may it never happen here.' She spat three times to ward off the evil eye.

'How come?' asked Aunt Zillah.

'Because a good Jew fears God, but a moneylender can't. If he did he wouldn't be a moneylender – it's forbidden in Talmud to lend for profit. Worse than murder.'

'Yes . . . Sure,' said Uncle Mendel. To Bernard: 'So who is this Einstein? Is he from Lodz and also a moneylender?'

Bernard seemed near to tears. 'I'm talking about Albert Einstein. He invented relativity.'

'An inventor yet,' said my mother impressed. 'So what is it?'

Bernard raised trembling fingers to his forehead as if to contain a near-bursting skull. 'L-look, Aunty Minnie, the greatest brains in the world don't understand the Theory of Relativity, so to expect me to explain it?'

'So why bring it up?' my mother demanded. 'And what's to do with Russia in the war?'

'It's . . . it's like this . . .' He took a deep breath. 'Political opinions is relative. Good or bad like anything else in life . . . Relative . . . Look, if you're . . . well, two people together for an hour. For one it can seem like a lifetime, for the other like five minutes. Or if you're in a synagogue a ten-minute sermon can also seem like five hours. You get me? It's relativity.'

My mother clicked her teeth, whistled, shook her head in wonderment, then said urgently to Mendel: 'There isn't a minute to lose.'

'Wassermatter?' asked her startled brother.

'We're a big family, no? (God be thanked). All over we got brothers, sisters, cousins, nephews, second and third cousins, in-laws, cousins two, three times removed – there must be thousands.'

'So?'

'So if this Einstein can make a living from it, with all the relatives we got you can make more than just a living. A fortune you'll make. And without having to do any inventing. A genus like you, a businessman, will soon learn the ins and outs. So first thing in the morning make a start.'

TEN

One afternoon Uncle Ben arrived home with a sack of coal over his shoulder. Asked by Granny Abrams where it came from, he explained: 'You can change Clothing Coupons for extra coal now, so I changed. I mean, what for should I want new clothes? And if I did want I can get second-hand down the Lane, which isn't on the ration.'

'You done a good job,' my mother agreed. 'We should all do similar. Save coal for the winter.'

Uncle Ben shook his head. 'This isn't for the heating.'

My mother: 'So what is it for? Making *lockshen* pudding? (Not that some people's don't taste like coal dust).'

'Scorched earth,' said Ben, and went on to explain how the German advance into the Soviet Union had led to the scorched earth policy. 'The same here. If them German *scheispots* come up the road I'll set fire to the place. And what burns better than coal? I'll get old buckets with holes in and fill with paper and wood with the coal on top and give them a warm welcome . . . Warm welcome,' he repeated with a giggle. 'Funny, eh?'

Granny Abrams stared at him, then shook her head. 'Funny? *Funny?* So far we been lucky, God be thanked. All over there's the bombing and people burned to cinders. So many names I can't even remember. Even Cousin Pearl, may she rest in peace. So what Hitler (may his daughters go blind) doesn't do, you'll finish off. Is that it? And that's funny?'

Aunt Zillah: 'He's funny all right. But not funny ha-ha; funny peculiar.'

My mother nodded. 'Strange how two brothers can be so different. Like they say in Yiddish: you don't need brains to have luck, but you need luck to have brains.'

Granny Abrams, grudgingly: 'Fair's fair. He wasn't so potty in the old days. Before he got that medal . . . But then again, could he have been sane in the first place to save the life from an officer?'

'Don't aggravate yourself,' said my mother soothingly. 'And you got to admit the idea of coal instead of clothes is not bad . . . Except I don't fancy second-hand from up the Lane. God alone knows what diseases was in them before . . . Is still in them. Hand-me-downs from the family is one thing, but from up the Lane?'

Ben, despite the discussion about him, had been quietly picking at the tulips on the wallpaper. He turned now with an enthusiastic: 'You got to do what we done in the trenches, Minnie. You run a bit of soap up the insides of the creases and joins, then go along them with a match. If there's any fleas or lice they go off pop.'

A collective shudder. 'Thank you very much,' said my mother. She wriggled her shoulders. 'It makes me itch all over even to think of. You got nothing better to talk about?'

'Sure,' said Ben. 'I was also thinking, apart from the scorched earth, about the Molotov cocktails. Like the Russians is using.'

My mother screwed up her face. 'Molotov I don't know. (Is he from round here?) But of cocktails I have heard. Mendel's been on enough about the Americans drinking them day and night in the bath. But being Russian I suppose they're from the vodka . . . And them Russians is sending?'

Granny Abrams: 'They couldn't send a drop kummel instead? For the digestion?'

'You're right,' Aunt Zillah agreed. 'Not that we got so much to digest these days. But what we have got certainly needs help.'

My mother's face went beetroot-red. 'You mean you can't digest my cooking all of a sudden? Is that it, you . . . you ungrateful cat?

If so, say out loud, and from now on you go do the shopping and cooking. Me – I'll go scrubbing. But to – to say that I, me, Minnie Ashe, can't cook . . .' A violent exhalation of breath. 'Of all the filthy things, that takes the cake – which, if you cook, will definitely take some digesting. So put that in your pipe and smoke it.'

'All I'm saying,' Aunt Zillah retorted hotly, 'is that the rubbish you get from the shops these days all the cooking in the world won't put right. That's all. But if you want to take umbrage . . .' an elaborate shrug '. . . go take.'

'Enough already!' Granny Abrams commanded.

'You got it wrong,' said Ben. 'These cocktails isn't for drinking, but for throwing at the Germans.'

My mother stared at him. 'I've heard some *meschuggener* things lately, but . . . but to throw at the Germans? You mean they'll be standing with mouths open for these cocktails and then fall down dead drunk?'

'You still got it wrong,' said Uncle Ben. 'It's not vodka in them. They're more like bombs. Made from petrol and paraffin and tar and things. I thought if I made a few we can all have, so if the Germans come up the road we can do like the Russians.'

Granny Abrams: 'Look, Benny, I know I'm

an old woman with her brain going soft, but you mean I got to go up to these filth (may they suffer the itch and be too paralysed to scratch) and ask them to please open the mouth while I—'

'Let me explain,' said Ben.

'Don't interrupt,' said his mother angrily. 'You know what for God gave us only one mouth but two ears? Because it's twice as important to listen. That's why. So tell me . . .' A *pah* of annoyance. 'Now I've forgotten what it was.'

'What I was trying to say,' Ben told her, 'was that 'cause they're bombs, like hand grenades, you throw them.'

'Throw?' my mother exclaimed. 'With my arthritis? And I also haven't enough to carry already? Specially with them gherkin things you're supposed to be making? I know you mean well, but be a good boy and leave winning the war to Eden and Churchill and the King England. If they want help, there's always Mendel.'

'Mendel's going to be busy enough,' said Uncle Ben with a wink. 'Me, too.'

My mother cocked her head suspiciously. 'Meaning?'

'Meaning that there's a shortage stockings.'

'I know there's a shortage stockings,' my mother replied.

Aunt Zillah groaned. 'What's he bought this time?'

'Soot,' Ben replied, and slid from the room before anyone could question him further.

Uncle Mendel's purchase was indeed sacks of soot: a rival dealer had bought them at the beginning of the war when, mixed with size, it was said by the Government to be the perfect dye for turning sheets, blankets and other materials into blackout curtains. The trouble was that people in the East End had neither sheets, blankets, nor other materials to spare for such an enterprise . . . and there was a shortage of size. So the soot had set solid in a dealer's shed until a use for it came to Uncle Mendel in the flash of an eyeball over a cup of tea in Berman's restaurant.

'This character was saying how, because of the shortage stockings, women is staining their legs with Oxo cubes dissolved in water. Turns them brown. Not a bad idea for Christian women.' Triumphantly: 'But because Oxo isn't made from Kosher beef, would Yiddisher women want to paint themselves with non-Kosher stockings? Huh? Does it make sense? Is it logic? Does it stand to reason? 'Course not! . . . But whoever heard of Kosher or non-Kosher soot? And these days what matters the colour stockings? Brown, black, yellow, pink – what difference? May my boils fester if I lie – a fortune I'll make! Just mix the soot with water and sell at a penny a leg and it's a million per cent profit. Like with Whatsit Gable when he got all that gold from the blackies for glass beads. I saw with my own eyeballs – beads! So why not soot? You wait and see.'

Mrs Klopps: 'So what about this powdered egg then?'

Mrs Block: 'I heard on the wireless. A diabolical liberty.'

Mrs Krenk: 'Why a liberty? You add this other stuff – the powdered milk – and a drop water and you got scrambled eggs. Without the milk you make with water and flour *lockshen*.'

My mother: 'So where's the chicken to make the soup to go with the *lockshen*? Eh? Answer me that . . . Powdered!' A dismissive *pshaw*! 'If it's egg it comes from chickens, no? In which case why turn to powder, to dust and ashes? Why not give the eggs? Likewise, what happens to the chickens? They also been turned into powder? And the cows? If so, why? If you ask me it's not all that meets the eye. There's something behind it.'

Mrs Block: 'Them with money is getting all right. Even the luxuries. I hear there was a woman got a banana the other day. Cost her five shillings.'

My mother: 'Five shillings! Never! I hope she choked on it.'

'She did,' said Mrs Block. 'On top of which her husband beat her black and blue for the wasted money.'

'Quite right, too,' said my mother.

'Talking about greengrocers and money reminds me,' said Mrs Krenk. 'We're supposed to be at war against the Germans and Fascists and anti-semites, but they're still about.'

'So long there's Jews there'll be Jew-haters,' my mother assured her bitterly.

'These kids – put up to it by their Mosleyite parents I suppose,' Mrs Krenk continued, 'started to get together outside Meyer Harris's shop in Commercial Street.'

'Meyer the greengrocer?' my mother asked. 'The one with the six fingers on the left hand.' With a nervous glance over her shoulder: 'They say it was because the mother was . . . well you know what, by the King of Darkness, may it never happen here.' Having spat three times to ward off the evil eye: 'Anyway, there's a funny story about him. He once said to my brother, Mendel the businessman, that he owed money left, right and centre and didn't know where it was going to come from. And Mendel said (and I was there, so I know for a fact), Mendel said: "Thank God for that." And Meyer said: "What's there to thank God for?" And Mendel said: "When you said you didn't know where it was going to come from. Otherwise you might have thought it was going to come from me." Funny, no?'

'No,' said Mrs Krenk, 'although this story about Meyer Harris is also about money. Like I was saying, them dirty kids stood outside the shop and shouted things like "Where's all the oranges and apples and bananas, Ikey Moe? Gone to the Black Market?" '

'They should be shot down like dogs then put to work,' said my mother with feeling.

'I was going to write a postcard, but Meyer Harris hit on the answer. He gave them each sixpence a day to do the shouting.'

'P-paid them? Sixpence a day?' My mother stared at her. 'T-to shout the anti-semitism?'

'He gone mad?' asked Mrs Klopps.

Mrs Krenk shook her head. 'After a week or so he told them he couldn't afford to pay them no longer. So they said they wasn't going to do it for nothing, and now he's left in peace and quiet.'

'Clever,' said Mrs Klopps. 'Like mine poor husband, the assistant caretaker, used to say, you catch more flies with jam than vinegar.'

'Just the same, the country's going to the dogs,' said Mrs Block miserably.

‘Then be grateful you don’t own it,’ my mother replied. ‘Though having had a butcher for a husband, she could own a few areas, like maybe Mayfair and Golders Green, eh girls?’

Unexpectedly, Mrs Block giggled.

‘What did I say that’s so funny?’ my mother demanded.

‘I remembered something Hymie, may he rest in peace, once told me: that since Adam had no neighbours it was no wonder he lived to be two hundred.’

Further bickering was avoided by the arrival of Benny Begel who informed us that if we wanted to get early in the queue, he’d heard that Solomons the fishmonger had taken delivery of a halibut the size of a dining room table which he was in the process of cutting into fair-shares-for-all portions.

I fancy tht neither powdered milk, powdered egg, Kosher Spam, nor peanut butter really found much favour with Uncle Mendel, but since they came from America they were automatically accepted as being preferable to the original foods from which they were derived.

‘It’s what in America the Yankees call the know-how,’ he explained. ‘I also got, but it needs the capital – and that I haven’t got. At least not yet . . . But you wait and see.’

'Powder reminds me,' said Aunt Zillah. 'What happened to them soot stockings? Not that I want none,' she added quickly.

Instead of the expected rage, Uncle Mendel's head described a series of short, sharp nods. 'Ahead of my time. That's what I am. Like with Pastor and the milk. *Oi veh*, how people suffered the consumption (may it never happen here) until Paul Muni (who was this Lew Pastor in the picture) done the milk.'

Ruth: 'I thought, Uncle Mendel, that a pastor was a sort of Christian religious leader.'

'Of course the leader!' Mendel retorted. 'What else if not the leader? Over in America the Christian pastor is like from here the Archbishop Canterbury. This one was called Lew: Lew the Pastor. You follow? Who invented the fresh milk for the consumption. And the aggravations he had! In a thousand years you'd never believe.'

A mirthless laugh from my mother. 'These days there isn't much I wouldn't believe . . . Still, if them Americans is so wonderful, a country filled with Christian wonder rabbis for the consumption, and if like you've said in the past they're full of the miracles and tickle tapes and is also full of Jews . . .' She paused for breath '. . . then why don't they do something to help us apart from sit and press the buttons and have fitted carpets and curtains in the lav? I know I'm not the one to ask, to question – but just for the sake of argument? . . . Eh? I know you're the businessman, the genus who goes regular to the pictures, but just the same: when you go to see this Eden, the Foreign Secretary (and the Americans aren't foreign all of a sudden?) go ask.'

After some thought Mendel said: 'I got on good authority, from the manager of the Troxy personal – and who better knows what's coming? – that them Yankee Doodles is on the way. Like with Tyrone Whosit who already come over to join the RAF and won Dunkirk with the Eagle Squadron. Take my word, and may my name be known to the police but forgotten by God if I lie, them Yanks is coming.'

As indeed they did come, to the greater glory of Uncle Mendel for his prescience, and I was taking a Sunday walk with him when sightseeing GIs were first spotted in Petticoat Lane.

Tears filled my uncle's eyes and slowly zig-zagged down the wrinkles of his cheeks as he tugged at my arm. After an elaborate sniff: 'L-look Simey. Look. S-see with your own eyeballs in black and white. A-Americans. Your actual Yankee Doodles. Here in London. In real life, like on the pictures. *Aie*, but this war'll be over in no time. You mark my words. Just look: see for yourself. They haven't been in the war five minutes, and they already got medal ribbons down to their knees. So if they can do that before they even come here, can you imagine what they'll do to the lousy, stinking Germans now they have come? Five minutes it'll take.'

'Shall we go and talk to them?' I asked.

Uncle Mendel frowned, then smiled. 'You're right. Introduce myself. After all, they're in the East End and who's more respected a name in the neighbourhood than Mendel Abrams?'

Shyly he led me to the stall where the Americans were contemplating second-hand bargains that included a Bakelite case for what had been an Ekco radio, a bound volume of *Boys' Own Paper*, one-sided Yiddish gramophone records, a stuffed cat in a glass case, a pair of what were claimed to be Kid Berg's boxing gloves, and an imitation parchment scroll of the Book of Esther. 'Interesting merchandise,' said Uncle Mendel enviously.

As we neared the GIs, Mendel straightened his jacket, adjusted his tie, stroked his wisps of hair into place and patted his boils. 'Hi, buddy-boys, as they say across the old . . . um . . . Herring Pond,' he began nervously in an appalling attempt at an American accent.

'So . . . um . . . well . . . how's with Edward Arnold and the old tickle tapes, eh? Still pressing the buttons to the White House? . . . *Aie, aie, aie*, Americans! Real Americans in the real flesh. It's – it's a real pleasure.' He took a deep breath, wiped his hand on his jacket, licked his lips and solemnly shook hands with the five GIs, giving a wink and a giggle to the Negro among them as he attempted a brief tap dance.

The Americans looked at Mendel, at each other, then back to my uncle. 'Yeah,' said one doubtfully. 'I'm fresh out of gum, but if you want cigarettes . . .' From a pocket he took a full packet and a near-full packet of Lucky Strikes.

'For me?' Mendel was wide-eyed as the cigarettes were pressed into his hands. 'The real, actual cigarettes like Humphrey smoked at the Gaumont?' He whistled. 'Nobody'll believe . . . By the way, I'm Mendel Abrams from round the corner in Zanzibar Terrace. I'm also in the big business like Edward and them other ones. Not that I grow the beef or the tinned salmon – at least not yet – but we're going to the good old US of A when this lousy war is over. And with you boys here it'll be over in no time. *Ach*, but I can't wait for the bathroom with the fitted carpets and the indoor lav with the music playing . . . I had an aunt come once from America (may she rest in peace), but she wasn't real American. More Polish . . . And what about them blonde secretaries? . . .'

Nervous excitement caused him to continue in this manner for some three minutes; a sort of twitchy stream of consciousness that embraced cowboys, Indians, Mickey Rooney, Lew Pastor, the Forest Rangers, death rays, Wall Street, the Donkey Serenade and the dirty dogs who tried to blow up the Statue of Liberty . . . 'And like I say, I'm going personal when this *vershtinkener* war is over,' he concluded breathlessly to the now open-mouthed, eye-bulging soldiers. He turned to the stall-holder and whispered: 'This is what they call making the contacts. Could be very useful to me' – and turned again to see the backs of the GIs as they hurriedly elbowed their way through the crowd.

Uncle Mendel made as though to go after them, but I put a hand on his sleeve and said: 'It's about time we went home. Mum'll be furious if we're late for lunch.'

He agreed, reluctantly, that we ought to return to Zanzibar Terrace, and we made our way there with my uncle beaming triumphantly and proudly holding the packets of Lucky Strike cigarettes to his chest as though he'd brought them direct from Mount Sinai.

His encounter with the Americans dominated the mealtime conversation ('and I'd've invited them here for tea later on, only they go drink the cocktails in the afternoon'), and inspired him to take every opportunity thereafter to introduce himself to the GIs who came sightseeing in and around Petticoat Lane. Many politely gave him their names and home addresses, presumably taking a chance that he would never actually pay a visit if and when he went to America; none, however, had time to spare to accompany him to Zanzibar Terrace for a cup of tea and a chat about Boris Karloff, heated swimming pools, the relative merits of Coney Island and Miami Beach, or J. Edgar Hoover, whom Mendel was convinced was a millionaire manufacturer of vacuum cleaners who did a bit of spying for Edward G. Robinson in his spare time.

One morning the hustle of washing and dressing was interrupted by a sudden series of truly terrifying screams. I rushed to the kitchen, as did other members of the household, to find my mother collapsed in a chair, white in the face, a letter clutched in trembling fingers. When she saw me, the screams turned to howls of anguish.

'W-w-wassermatter?' asked Uncle Mendel.

'Matter? *Matter?!*' She waved the letter at

him. 'R-read and you'll see what's the matter.'

The letter was addressed to me, but my mother had opened it on the principle that I couldn't possibly have any secrets from her, and if I did it was her duty to discover what was going on. It held no secrets: simply an instruction that I was to register for service with the Armed Forces.

When she'd been near-calmed by several cups of tea, my mother's agony reduced to a rhythmic sobbing. 'As if I didn't have enough aggravations, enough heartaches already, now they want to take my baby away from me.'

Uncle Mendel: 'But all over the country, Minnie, people is being called up by the million. Haven't enough of our own nephews and cousins' children gone?'

'So they can't manage with just one less?' my mother retorted. 'It's not sufficient to be a widow?' She took a handkerchief from an apron pocket, vigorously blew her nose and addressed herself to the ceiling. 'You take away mine husband (may he rest happy in Paradise), but that's not enough, eh? You got to be greedy. My darling son, just a little boy, You also got to take. So why not be done with it and take the lot of us? Me, Ruthie – everybody? If You want to kill me, do it quick, not drive me to the grave with aggravations. What You got against me, huh? Just say. Explain. Tell me what I done that's so terrible . . .' She shrugged. 'It's like talking to a brick wall.'

'All of a sudden I'm your little darling son?' I asked. 'I thought I was a Cossack and a toerag and a dog's-body and a mother killer and God alone knows what else.'

A grudging: 'You might have grown out of it. Brought me joy for mine old age. But with my luck you'll go get yourself killed just to aggravate me, you selfish swine, so even that I'll be denied.'

'What you going to put down for?' asked Uncle Ben. Hopefully: 'The Army? The Middlesex Regiment like me?'

'God forbid!' my mother screamed. 'With the trenches and the mud and the lice? Is that what you want, you madman? It's all I'm short of.'

'It's not so bad these days,' said Uncle Mendel. 'I saw on the newsreel at the pictures only the other day. They go for marches in the country – and what could be healthier with all that marvellous fresh air – and sing "There'll Always Be An England", play ludo and snakes and ladders and eat like the Duke from Westminster. May I never move from this room alive and then be cursed with a black year – the Duke Westminster. I seen with my own eyeballs.'

My mother nodded. 'But who does the cooking? . . . No, the Army I don't fancy.'

'So what about the Navy?' asked Aunt Zillah.

My mother shuddered. 'All that water? The damp? *Oi, oi, oi*, he'll get the rheumatism within the fortnight. And them ships can leak. To let in the cholera and all the other filth you get from the rivers. 'Cause doesn't the rivers empty into the sea? Didn't I read? . . . And remember what happened to the *Titanic*, which was also a ship. I also read about – just last week in the *Empire News*.'

'That was sunk by an iceberg,' I said.

'Eisenberg?' asked Granny Abrams, cupping a hand round an ear.

'Iceberg,' said Uncle Ben.

Granny Abrams shrugged. 'Eisenberg, Iceberg, Goldberg . . . They'll always find some Yiddisher person to put the blame on.'

Ruth: 'That leaves the RAF. You could be a Spitfire or a bomber pilot.'

'Up in the air!' my mother shrieked. 'Up in the air? It can be very dangerous, you know that? You should know better, being the big nob in the Cross. Airplanes yet! It isn't natural . . . Not that anything is these days,' she admitted with a grimace. 'Just the same, flying. In the air.'

'There was another thousand-bomber raid

on Germany last night,' said Ben. 'I heard on the wireless.'

'That I certainly don't fancy,' said my mother vehemently. 'Flying over Germany? Dropping bombs? Them lousy Germans can be very spiteful.'

'So what's left?' asked Aunt Zillah with a sigh.

'Left? *Left?!*' my mother shrilled. 'You should ask what's right more like. And the answer to that is that nothing's right.'

'Anyone want my opinion?' I asked.

'Opinion?' my mother screamed. 'Since when have you been entitled to an opinion, you guttersnipe? Here we all are working out the best way for you to be killed . . .' In a small voice: 'Killed' as though suddenly aware of the implications of it all. 'My little dolly,' she croaked, and collapsed into a threnodic grizzle.

'There's the Bevin Boys,' said Uncle Mendel. 'I saw on the pictures.'

'On the pictures? Bevin Boys?' asked my mother hopefully between sniffs. 'What's them?'

'Ernie Bevin. Minister Labour. There's the shortage miners, so instead of the Services, kids can go down the mines. Dig coal.'

'Coal!' my mother howled. 'You're as potty as your brother, and that's saying something.

Coal? Down there? Underground? With the damp and consumption? And the piles?'

'Maybe I'll fail my medical,' I offered.

My mother, hopefully: 'Maybe in a place damp like this, and previous Kilburn, piles you already got.' Thoughtfully: 'There's the flat feet, the fallen arches, the palpitations . . . To say nothing of the softening of the brain and the phlegm, God forbid . . . I only wish now I hadn't fed you so good . . . My little boy, taken away from me left, right and centre.'

Granny Abrams: 'Maybe you can get Dr Lee arrange some disease. Nothing serious, but a few shillings-worth.'

Uncle Ben: 'Lee? With three sons in the Army?'

Granny Abrams: 'His own sons? I always did say he wasn't up to much as a doctor. I don't know why we still go to him. For years I've seen him and he still says he can find nothing wrong . . . And that's a doctor?'

'A liberty,' my mother agreed. 'And to think that for that you pay good money.'

Granny Abrams shrugged. 'Pay? Who pays? When he finds something wrong with me, so then I'll pay. But to pay him for not finding nothing? I'm not that mad.'

I registered for the safest role I could think of: RAF ground crew, but was summoned at the end of 1943 for service with the Royal Navy. Uncle Ben drove everyone mad by his nonstop whistling of 'Hearts of Oak': Uncle Mendel advised me to take up tap dancing like Fred Astaire who could have been an admiral at the Mile End Hippodrome if it hadn't been for Ginger Whatsit; Aunt Zillah urged me go as quickly as possible for the sake of peace and quiet; my mother passed the days before my departure in a state of near-mourning.

'If only your poor father was alive, he'd know what to do. Be able to advise. But who is there? Even Mendel, for all him being the family genus, can't come up with a solution. Maybe we should go see the rabbi. If we was back in Kilburn, Iron Foot Yossell could've cut the cards. Or there's Solly Litvak's son, who's learning to be a solicitor. Or Mrs Krenk could perhaps write a postcard.'

'Much good that lot would do,' I replied. 'All over the country – all over the world – people are being called up for the Services. Why should I be an exception?'

'But in the Navy yet,' my mother wailed. 'Why couldn't they've put you somewhere safe?'

'What's safe these days? . . . Anyway, the war might be over before they get round to me.'

'Not with my luck . . . Although I'll never

know what I've done to deserve it,' she added, shaking a fist at the ceiling. 'But if your father, may he rest in peace, was alive, things might've been different. Perhaps we'd have maybe had the money to 'prentice you to learn a proper trade. Something that meant you didn't have to go in the rotten Navy. Like the tailoring or cabinet-making or the hairdressing.'

'What makes you think they're not called up?'

'You trying to tell me we're all walking about naked (God forbid) because all the tailors is in this Navy thing? Likewise, who's making the coffins for all the people being killed left, right and centre (may it never happen here) if not the cabinet-makers? And we've also got our hair to our knees because the barbers is all catching rheumatism on the water? Does it make sense? Does it stand to reason? For a boy who had his *bar mitzvah* you talk a lot of rubbish.'

Nobody slept much on the night before my departure for Portsmouth: at first because of my mother's noisy weeping, then because the communication of her misery caused everyone else to join in. As Aunt Zillah put it between sobs: 'Anyone would think it wasn't already damp enough down here. If there was sunshine we'd have a rainbow.'

In the morning, after we'd washed and dressed and had a tear-garnished breakfast, my mother produced my familiar carrier bag – and two extra. 'There's the *lockshen* soup left from yesterday. Not as strong as I'd like, but what can you do these days? Portsmouth must be miles away, and God alone knows when you'll eat next (or what rubbishy muck they'll give you), so I also put in my Thermos. Also *lockshen* soup. Then there's extra sandwiches – I'm afraid cheese and that powdered egg filth, and *wurst* like red bread was all I can manage – and some biscuits. Also the chocolate ration. There's also a change of socks and underwear.'

She'd been fighting back the tears, but they came now as she went on: 'I also packed your father's prayer shawl and prayer books. I don't know if there's any Yiddisher people in this Portsmouth, or if them ships have synagogues, but a prayer from time to time might come in handy. Won't do no harm, anyway.'

'The best synagogue is in the heart,' said Granny Abrams.

'Since when has this dog's-body had a heart?' my mother demanded. 'Let him rely better on bricks and mortar . . . I've also packed a photo of your poor father, and a selection from other members of the family. Up in the hall there's an umbrella and your mac and your wellingtons, and one of Mendel's old bowler hats: with all the water about – and what's the sea if not water? – you'll need all the protection you can get . . . So what else is there? There's the bandages and iodine and Ex-Lax and gas mask and things, and also bicarb, because God forbid the cooking you're going to have. Also a packet soda for the insect bites and a bit of that paint of Mendel's for the gassing. And there's Lysol. On a ship with all them strange people is as bad as down the shelters – the phlegm and consumption and fleas, and who's to know what else?, God forbid!'

'I-I'm supposed to take this to Portsmouth?'

'Of course take. What else if not take?'

'I'll need a lorry,' I protested.

'I'll take on the barrow to Waterloo Station,' said Uncle Ben.

'That's the other side London,' Mendel roared, 'and you're supposed to collect that consignment piano keys . . . The ivory must be worth a fortune,' he explained with a wink – then shrugged. 'So OK, give Simey a hand with his belongings. And talking of the piano keys reminds me: practise with the tap dancing, eh?'

'Be a good boy,' said Aunt Zillah.

'Send a picture postcard of them foreign places,' said Ruth.

'Foreign?!' my mother cried. 'You mean he's going foreign? Like from abroad? Nobody told me about foreign. *Oi veh!* He could end up on some island like I read in the *Daily Mirror* – eaten alive by wild animals and put in the cooking pot and worshipped as a White God . . .' She managed a laugh. 'Of that there's no chance . . . But foreign! *Aie, aie, aie* . . . Why can't he just sail up and down outside Westcliff or Brighton in the fresh air to stop them *scheispot* Germans coming? Why foreign? If the Germans want to invade, what good's it going to do being foreign? Mendel, you must put a stop to it.'

'It's time to go,' I said quickly.

'G-go?' my mother stammered. 'So soon. Without a bowl soup? The war won't wait five minutes?'

'The train won't,' I replied.

'Catch the next one.'

'They'll shoot him for a deserter,' said Uncle Ben.

'Sh-shoot? *Oi gevult!* So go! Go! Quick – there isn't a minute to lose!'

As I led the way to the front door, Granny Abrams said: 'And don't go saving the life from no officer. Or you'll end up like that one.'

Tears . . . Kisses . . . The front door slammed.

Grasping the handles of his barrow, Uncle Ben whispered: 'Don't worry, Simey, I'll get rid of all this for you.' We made our way along Zanzibar Terrace – and it seemed as though my mother's howls of despair were still with me.

They were.

At the corner of Commercial Road I turned my head to see her in apron and bedroom slippers running after us, shouting to bemused onlookers: 'It's my baby boy! . . . A toerag, but all I got! . . . They're taking him to the Navy! . . . And foreign yet! . . . So don't just stand like stuffed dummies – do something . . . Go call the police! Fetch a doctor! . . . Write a postcard! . . . Tell the Mayor Stepney! . . .'

She stopped, exhausted, in the middle of the road, shook her fists at the heavens and sobbed her heart out.